Andrew D. White, Victor Chauffour-Kestner, Archibald Young

Ulrich von Hutten

imperial poet and orator - the great knightly reformer of the 16th century

Andrew D. White, Victor Chauffour-Kestner, Archibald Young

Ulrich von Hutten
imperial poet and orator - the great knightly reformer of the 16th century

ISBN/EAN: 9783337294793

Printed in Europe, USA, Canada, Australia, Japan

Cover: Foto ©Andreas Hilbeck / pixelio.de

More available books at **www.hansebooks.com**

ULRICH VON HUTTEN,

𝔍𝔪𝔭𝔢𝔯𝔦𝔞𝔩 𝔓𝔬𝔢𝔱 𝔞𝔫𝔡 𝔒𝔯𝔞𝔱𝔬𝔯;

THE GREAT KNIGHTLY REFORMER OF THE 16TH CENTURY.

TRANSLATED FROM

CHAUFFOUR-KESTNER'S ÉTUDES SUR LES RÉFORMATEURS
DU 16ME SIÈCLE,

BY

ARCHIBALD YOUNG, ESQ.,

ADVOCATE.

EDINBURGH:
T. & T. CLARK, 38, GEORGE STREET.
LONDON: HAMILTON, ADAMS, AND CO.

MDCCCLXIII.

MURRAY AND GIBB, PRINTERS, EDINBURGH.

TRANSLATOR'S PREFACE.

IR JAMES STEPHEN remarks, in one of his admirable Essays on Ecclesiastical Biography, that 'English literature is singularly defective in whatever relates to the Reformation in Germany and Switzerland, and to the lives of the great men by whom it was accomplished;' and to none of these great men does this observation more forcibly apply than to Ulrich von Hutten, of whose varied and eventful life, and powerful influence both upon the revival of letters and the reformation of religion in the sixteenth century, no account is to be found in our language, beyond the brief and imperfect notices afforded by magazine articles and biographical dictionaries. Yet scarcely any career in that stirring century is more diversified by adventures, or more surrounded by strong elements of dramatic interest. The eldest son of an ancient and noble family of Franconia—whose knighthood was esteemed the flower of German chivalry—and gifted with remarkable abilities,

Ulrich von Hutten might have attained to the highest dignities in church or state, if he could have been content to follow the old paths, and accept the established order of things. But he preferred to be a champion and a martyr in the cause of civil and religious liberty. When a mere lad, he fled from the cloister of Fulda, in order to escape being compelled to embrace a monastic life, as he thought that, in some other career, he could better serve God and his country. Afterwards, he gave up to his family the estate which fell to him, as eldest son, on his father's death, that they might not be involved in the proscription and ruin which he was about to incur by the publication of the *Trias Romana*,—that tremendous satire upon the manifold corruptions of Rome, beside whose withering sarcasm and terrible invective, the attacks of About, and other modern assailants of the Papacy, sound tame and feeble. At twenty-eight, he had written the *Epistolæ Obscurorum virorum*, the national satire of Germany, which, according to the celebrated Herder, effected for Germany incomparably more than Hudibras for England, or Gargantua for France, or the Knight of La Mancha for Spain. It gave the victory to Reuchlin over the begging friars, and to Luther over the court of Rome. At thirty-five he died, a worn-out, persecuted, destitute fugitive, on the little green island of Uffnau, in the Lake of Zurich, almost within the shadow of the mighty Alps,—finishing his life and his work at an age when some of the world's greatest men, such as Mahomet, Luther, and Oliver Cromwell, had scarcely begun theirs. Yet in that short, but busy and fruitful life, how much had been accomplished, amidst poverty, persecution, privations and anxieties of all kinds, and frequent travel! Hutten's works amount to about fifty separate publications, in prose and verse, many of which deeply stirred the German mind, and materially contributed to the triumph of the Reformation over the papal power, and of polite learning over the old scholastic teaching. It is surely somewhat remarkable, that there is no life of such a man in the English language. There are several biographies of him in French; and in German—as might naturally be expected—a great number, of which the latest and most complete is that by Dr Friederich Strauss. I have attempted, in some measure, to supply this want in our literature by translating M. V. Chaffour-Kestner's life of the great knightly reformer of Germany, to which my attention was first directed when writing an article on Ulrich von Hutten for the 'Eclectic Review' of July 1858. This biography is very appropriately dated from Zurich, where Hutten found a last refuge, when all others had failed him, beside the intrepid and noble-minded Zwingle. It contains,

within a brief compass, a picturesque and popular
narrative of Hutten's chequered career; and, as far
as possible, makes him speak for himself, through
the medium of those among his works which exercised the greatest influence on his era, and which
best illustrate his character and designs.   Such are
the philippics against Ulrich, Duke of Wurtemburg,
who had assassinated his cousin, Hans von Hutten;
his edition of the work of Laurentius Valla, im-
pugning the donation of Constantine to the Holy
See, dedicated, with characteristic audacity, to Pope
Leo X.,—a book which had a powerful influence in
convincing Luther of the antichristian nature of the
papal power; the *Trias Romana*, the most terrible
exposure ever made of the vices and corruptions
of the Roman court; the dialogues entitled, *The
Monitor* and *The Brigands*; and the Letters to
the Emperor Charles V., and to the Elector Frederick, the friend and protector of Luther.   These
works are largely drawn upon by M. Chauffour-
Kestner, and his quotations from them give a vivid
idea both of the character of Hutten and of the
age in which he lived.   Of Hutten, with his restless
impetuosity often bordering upon rashness, his intense activity of thought and action, his disinterest-
edness, his sincerity and love of truth, his bitter
hatred of every form of oppression, his fervent devotion to freedom and to the fatherland;—of the age in

which he lived, with its deeply-felt wants and aspirations, its sense of ignorance and oppression, and its strivings after clearer vision and healthier life.

No man was ever more thoroughly a type, an epitome, of his age, than Ulrich von Hutten. Many phases of that age have been better represented by others—its scholarship by Reuchlin and Erasmus, its religious reformation by Luther and Melancthon, its knighthood by Franz von Sickingen. But no one presents so many of its aspects in his single person as Hutten, who was at once knight, scholar, poet, and reformer. His marvellous activity of thought, and variety and fertility of invention, form another marked peculiarity of his genius, which has been finely pointed out by Von Ranke. ' Hutten,' he says, ' is not a great scholar, nor is he a very profound thinker; his excellence lies more in the exhaustlessness of his vein, which gushes forth with equal impetuosity, equal freshness, in the most varied forms—in Latin and in German, in prose and in verse, in eloquent invective and in brilliant satirical dialogue. Nor is he without the spirit of acute observation : here and there— for example, in the *Nemo*—he soars to the bright and clear regions of genuine poetry. His hostilities have not that cold malignant character which disgusts the reader; they are always connected with a cordial devotion to the side he advocates; he leaves on the mind an impression of perfect veracity, of uncompromising frankness and honesty; above all, he has always great and single purposes which command universal sympathy; he has earnestness of mind, and a passion—to use his own words—"for godlike truth, for common liberty." '

Hutten has been accused of rashness, of a revolutionary spirit, of a tendency to precipitate matters before the proper time had arrived; and perhaps there is some truth in this accusation. Yet it ought to be remembered that reformation, on the basis of the existing ecclesiastical institutions, was impracticable, and that the quiet and gradual development of reformation, even on the basis of the Bible, was no less impossible. Force, in the first instance, was used by Rome to prevent and arrest such a development, which would have been most agreeable to the Reformers themselves; and the only way to win the right of free inquiry and free action, was to meet force by force. The Reformers, before the Reformation, had tried the power of persuasion, and their voices had been silenced by the sword and the stake. It remained to abandon all hope of civil and religious freedom, to submit for ever to the bondage of Rome, or to make use of the right of resistance, and, like Ulrich von Hutten, to draw the sword and fling away the scabbard. The cause was just and holy; and the blood shed to maintain it rests on the heads of those who strove to crush it by force, not on those who perilled fortune and life to secure its triumph.

I have said that scarcely any life of the sixteenth century presents stronger elements of dramatic interest than that of Hutten. His early flight from the Abbey of Fulda; his travels, as a poor scholar and student, throughout Germany and the neighbouring countries—now the guest of a peasant or burgher, now of a powerful noble or wealthy bishop, whose hospitality he repaid by his verses and by the charms of his conversation; his perils from shipwreck and robbers; his first journey into Italy, during which he was besieged in his lodgings at Pavia by French soldiers, and reduced to such straits, that he gave himself up for lost, and, like a true poet, composed his own epitaph; his escape, and subsequent enlistment in the army of Maximilian; his return to Germany, and publication of those eloquent philippics against Duke Ulrich of Wurtemburg, whereby he elevated his private wrong, in the assassination of his cousin, into an affair of national importance; his second visit to Italy, and his combat, single-handed, against five Frenchmen, who had insulted Kaiser Maximilian and the fatherland; his coronation at Augsburg, as Imperial Poet and Orator, by the Emperor's own hand; his brilliant services at the head of that

noble army of scholars, the friends and followers of
Reuchlin, who emancipated the human mind from
the bondage of the old scholastic teaching; his
terrible assaults upon the vices and corruptions of
Rome; his heroic self-abnegation in giving up his
patrimony to his family, lest they should suffer by
his proscription; his friendship with Sickingen,
and their evenings in the strong castle of Ebernberg,
passed in reading the writings of Luther, till the
strong hand of the Bayard of Germany grasped to
his war-sword, and he exclaimed, ' It is the cause
of God and of truth!   It is our fatherland which
commands us to listen to the counsels of Luther and
of Hutten, and to defend the true faith;' last scene
of all, the defeat and death of Sickingen, the proscription of Hutten, his flight to Basle, Mulhausen,
and Zurich, and his early death on the little island
of Uffnau;—where is the romance that possesses
stronger or more varied elements of dramatic interest than this true story of one of the countless
champions and martyrs of freedom?   One poet at
least—Frölich of Aarau, in Switzerland—has felt
this, and has composed a poem in seven cantos,
entitled ' Ulrich von Hutten.'

The works by which Hutten roused the national
mind of Germany, and won the battles of freedom,
may now lie almost forgotten on the shelves of
libraries, as the war-swords and panoply of the

knights of that age now serve only as memorials on the walls of armouries and arsenals. Not because there remain no abuses to overthrow, no enemies to overcome; but because the style of our writing has changed, as well as the fashion of our warfare. Yet not the less, on that account, should we value the weapons with which these sixteenth century Reformers fought and won the great victory whose fruits we are now enjoying. As to Hutten himself, it has been finely said by one of his German biográphers, that 'his arrows are immortal; and wherever in German lands a battle is gained against obscurantism and spiritual tyranny, against priestcraft and despotism, there have Hutten's weapons been.'

I am far from holding out the work of M. Chauffour-Kestner as a perfect or complete biography of Ulrich von Hutten. But it certainly furnishes a better account of the great German patriot—the representative of the political aspect of the Reformation —than any to be found in the English language; and I shall consider my labour in translating it amply repaid, if I shall succeed in inducing some abler writer to undertake a fuller and more complete biography of one, whose sufferings and services in the cause of freedom deserve to be more generally known among us.

EDINBURGH, *January* 1863.

AUTHOR'S PREFACE.

ALL liberties are sisters; or rather there is but one liberty, the indomitable daughter of conscience. The progress of civilisation consists in disengaging liberty from the yoke of nature and from the yoke of institutions, in making of each man a man, in conquering for all the full and perfect exercise of their physical, intellectual, and moral faculties. In that divine progression of history, each ruin which is made in the ancient slavery, announces and prepares a new ruin. It is therefore that those who, in the sixteenth century, affirmed that *all Christians are brothers*, are the legitimate ancestors of those who, in the eighteenth century, declared that *all men are equal*.

In that long infancy of liberty, during the ages of which the great battles are termed Christianity, Reformation, Revolution, the Reformation has had the honour of reclaiming and reconquering for liberty her very sanctuary—the conscience. But we need not go beyond our own time to seek for examples in that memorable epoch. We have lately seen liberty driven from the arena which she filled with her mighty voice : she has retired into her sanctuary, and from that prolific retreat she will emerge stronger, more serious, more self-assured, to march onward to new triumphs. Let the weak despair : it is the consequence and the punishment of their feebleness. But it must not, cannot be, that the strong themselves should falter and lose heart; for liberty shall not perish. Who can tell all the storms to which she has been exposed! How often has she been battered by the winds, and abandoned on the waves like a dismasted vessel! And ere long she again wooed the breeze, more beautiful and more majestic than ever! But she demands from her defenders an undaunted spirit, a fearless heart. She despises the cowards who believe her dead, because they dare not raise her from the tomb, where they pretend that she sleeps for ever, but where she only slumbers for a time. She has nought to do with tears and lamentations : she requires deeds, and the fiery words which give birth to action.

I believe that I have found such words in the writings of Hutten; and I repeat them to my contemporaries, happy if they cherish or rekindle in some hearts a spark of the sacred fire which has animated so many heroes.

ZURICH, 29th July 1852.

ULRICH VON HUTTEN.*

I.

ULRICH VON HUTTEN was born on the 21st April 1488, of one of the noblest families of Franconia—of that country where every man was noble. From the tenth century the Huttens had acquired an honourable name in camp and council; and at the commencement of the sixteenth, they had thirty knights in the service of the Empire. The Franconian nobility were, at that period, considered the most perfect type of German chivalry. They had preserved their independence after the formation of the territorial principalities; and when, almost everywhere else, the lesser nobility had been, willingly or by force, subjected to the sovereignty of the princes, they owned allegiance only to the Empire,—that is

* Several notes have been added by the translator, relating to the less generally known of the eminent persons mentioned by M. Chauffour-Kestner, in order to enable the reader intelligently to follow the progress of the narrative without going beyond the volume in his hand. These notes have been placed together at the end of the volume, and each note is indicated by its number on the page to which it refers.

to say, to an idea rather than to a reality. They
formed a sort of noble democracy, which properly
took its place by the side of the middle class
democracy of the towns, and which, not less than
the latter, was pervaded by a remarkable spirit of
liberty, joined to a profound sentiment of national
unity.

The castle of Steckelberg, the residence of the
Huttens, was situated some leagues distant from
Fulda, on the confines of Franconia and Hesse.
It was one of the feudal residences of which Hutten
has left us the description: 'Our castles are con-
structed, not for pleasure, but security. All is
sacrificed to the necessity of defence. They are
contracted between ramparts and ditches; armouries and stables usurp the place of apartments.
Everywhere the smell of powder, horses, cattle, the
noise of dogs and oxen, and, upon the margin of
the mighty forests which surround us, the cries of
wolves. Always agitation; perpetual coming and
going: our gates, open to all, often permit assassins
and thieves to enter. Each day there is a new
care. If we maintain our independence, we risk
being crushed among too powerful enemies; if we
put ourselves under the protection of some prince,
we are forced to espouse his quarrels. We cannot
sally forth without an escort. In order to hunt, or
to visit a neighbour, we must don casque and

cuirass.   Always, everywhere, war.'   War, in fact, even to the end, was the normal state of feudal society.   Hutten, as we shall see, did not detest it ; but he wished it to be ennobled by its aim, and by the grandeur of the results achieved.

----♦----

II.

E know nothing of the infancy of Hutten ; but we can fancy what it must have been, in the midst of the savage manners of which we have just sketched the picture.   At eleven years of age, his parents sent him to the school of the Abbey of Fulda.   They had four sons ; and, although Ulrich was the eldest, they thought that he would best make his way in the world by the convent, as he was of delicate constitution, and of short stature in that family of giants.   Hutten learned with ardour and success all that they could teach him in the celebrated school of the Abbey, and especially the rudiments of the classical languages ; but he acquired no taste for a monastic life.   'Having seen the world' (he says at a subsequent period), 'it appeared to me that, in another condition, I could live in a manner more pleasing to God, and more useful to men.'   Thenceforward,

B

with that decisive and courageous resolution which
does not compound with duty, his mind was made
up.   Nothing could induce him to become a monk.

He was emboldened in his resistance by his fellow-
student, Crotus Rubianus (1), who remained his
friend, and by Eitelwolf von Stein (2), who was his
most useful protector. The latter addressed himself at first to the parents of the young man, and
entreated them not to force his inclinations. He
found them deaf to entreaties, and, conjecturing the
cause of their resistance, he went to the Abbot of
Fulda, and addressed him in the following terms :
' Are you not ashamed to destroy so promising a
genius ?' The experienced statesman had already
divined in the youthful scholar the great man of
the future ; but the monk had made the same dis-
covery, and was not less ardent in his efforts to
secure him. He endeavoured to dazzle his eyes by
the dignities and honours which a monastic career
would place within his reach. Hutten remained
immovable. He had then recourse to menaces ;
but these only rendered Hutten the more determined. Then the Abbot called in his parents.
The father laid his commands upon him, and swore
that, if he did not obey, he would see him no more :
the mother wept and entreated. But the loyalty
of young Hutten's nature forbade him to sacrifice
the instinctive dictates of his conscience either to

ambition or fear, or to the natural affections, which were always so strong in his heart. To escape from further persecutions, he fled from Fulda. He was then sixteen years old.

Bitter but salutary initiation into the great battle of life! Later, other seductions will be tried, other dangers will threaten him; but in that first temptation he acquired the necessary strength of character. After what he then suffered, it will cost him nothing to remain faithful to the voice of conscience. His family for a long time was lost to him. His father no longer wished either to see him, or to interest himself in his affairs.

-----◆-----

III.

N leaving the Abbey, Hutten at first went to Erfurth, where he might see Luther; but he soon afterwards repaired to Cologne, where he was rejoined by his friend Crotus Rubianus. Cologne was the most ancient and illustrious of the German universities; and the two youths arrived there, full of ardour in the pursuit of knowledge.

Knowledge! But what kind of knowledge? The scholastic system still reigned supreme; and dialectics were the first branch of study to which they applied themselves. 'We learn to fulminate arguments, to overwhelm each other with syllogistic strokes, to maintain up to thirty propositions, to prove the for and against.' Futile and wretched training, which, instead of exercising and rectifying the intellect, perverted it, and sent it forth on a wrong path! However, that study was not lost: the scholar, later in life, will avail himself of the teaching of his masters, in his great and triumphant controversy with the theologians of Cologne.

But the natural integrity of his disposition did not permit Hutten to stray long in these devious paths. He soon yielded to the inclination which led him towards classical antiquity. He was the assiduous and favourite pupil of Ragius Æsticampius (3), who, in opposition to the old science of the Scholastics, taught, with great success, the new science of languages and ancient literature. It was the invincible tendency of the epoch. The time was approaching when the human spirit would burst the swaddling clothes which had protected its infancy, but which had for a long time impeded its growth and development. In order to prepare for this decisive struggle against the iron slavery of the Middle Ages, the modern world sought its best arms in classical antiquity. What, in truth, could they do better than invoke the calm and clear reason of the Greeks, the practical good sense of the Romans, against that mass of subtleties, of shadows which obscured the light?

But the old world, the old science, were not willing to give place. We shall afterwards see what blows it was necessary to strike, in order to achieve for classical learning a little air and liberty. The theologians of Cologne launched against Ragius the accusation which was fatal to Socrates, the eternal accusation with which all science is met at its first appearance. They accused him of being an innovator, a corrupter of youth, and expelled him from the University. Later, we shall find them again animated by the same passions ; but the times will be changed, and their blind hatred will shatter itself against the holy league of good sense, of learning, and of wit.

Ragius carried his teaching to Frankfort-on-the-Oder, where the Margrave of Brandenburgh was about to found a university. Hutten followed him. He was appointed one of the first masters, and requited by his earliest poem the hospitality which he received.

IV.

FROM 1506 to 1514, Ulrich von Hutten only appears at long intervals. He set out on his travels in order to finish his education. Like Ulysses, to whom his contemporaries have often compared him, he had to endure the buffetings of the waves, the treachery of men, and the persecutions of a contrary destiny. He first visited the north of Europe ; later, he appears at Rostock, at Wittemberg, at Vienna, sowing broad-cast on his way much admired poetical compositions. These travels, undertaken without resources, were often full of great hardships. On the Baltic, he was exposed to a frightful tempest ; in Pomerania, in that country of the Cyclops, as one of his friends says, he was robbed of his slender baggage. He travelled in the style of knights-errant—or as the students of Germany have done for so long a period—trusting to chance, on foot, living on alms, without anxiety or thought for the future, certain of always finding some abbot, or lover of good verses, or the hospitable table of a peasant. Sometimes the charms of his conversation procured for him a flattering reception. At Olmutz, for example, the Bishop, after having lodged him for several days, and treated him magnificently, gave him, on his departure, a horse and some money.

In 1512, Hutten was at Pavia, at the time when
the French defended that town, besieged by the
Swiss. His sojourn there was, for our hero, a suc-
cession of misfortunes. Having got into a quarrel
with some soldiers of the garrison, he had to endure
from them, in his small student's lodging, a siege
in form. He gave up all hope, prepared to die as
became a poet, and composed a beautiful epitaph
for himself in Latin. When the town was taken,
he expected to have been set free; but the victors,
pretending to take him for a German in the service of France, under that pretext, maltreated and
plundered him. He hastened to fly from that
unhappy town, and took refuge at Bologna.
Misery, however, seemed to dog his steps; and his
necessities became so pressing, that he enlisted as
a common soldier in Maximilian's army. 'If I were
to tell you what I suffered in Italy' (he afterwards
says to his friend Perckheimer (4)), 'you would
hear a tragedy so wonderful and melancholy, that
you would scarcely believe me.' This, however,
did not hinder him from making verses in honour
of the Empire, and against its enemies. On his return, his friends pressed him to dedicate them to
Maximilian : he did so, but in so haughty a tone,
that it was impossible to mistake him for a courtier.

He derived no advantage either from the verses
or the dedication; but Eitelwolf von Stein recom-

mended him to the Archbishop of Mayence, Albert of Brandenburg, who received and treated him as a friend. He composed a poem in his honour, which is considered one of his best works in Latin verse. He allowed it to be printed only at the request of his patron, and with marked repugnance. 'If I could refuse you anything, certainly I would not have consented to that. You know to what risk I expose myself. You know the ideas and the customs of the German nobility: one would take them for centaurs rather than knights. If a young man applies himself to the study of the sciences, they point at him the finger of scorn, as a degenerate being, as a disgrace to his family and nobility. Thus several who were making good progress have turned back, and have bowed the neck to the yoke of prejudice. Are we not condemned each day to hear these centaurs exclaim that they are the pillars of the country, that in them alone is true nobility, and that they alone are qualified for great exploits both in peace and war?'

I take notice of that first expression of a complaint which often recurs in the writings of Hutten. He reproaches the German nobility with their coarseness, drunkenness, and contempt for the arts and sciences. One object of his ambition was to combat and destroy that prejudice of the nobility, which considered the cultivation of literature as a mark of low birth.   Every noble of the sixteenth century was proud of his nobility; Hutten often speaks with complaisance of the distinction of his family; but from a feeling then entirely new, he was still more proud of personal distinction : ' I attach little importance' (he writes to Perckheimer) ' to the nobility which arises merely from the accident of birth, and with which there is combined no personal merit.   For my part, I would wish to ennoble myself, and to transmit to my descendants some distinction which I have not inherited from my ancestors.'

<hr />

V.

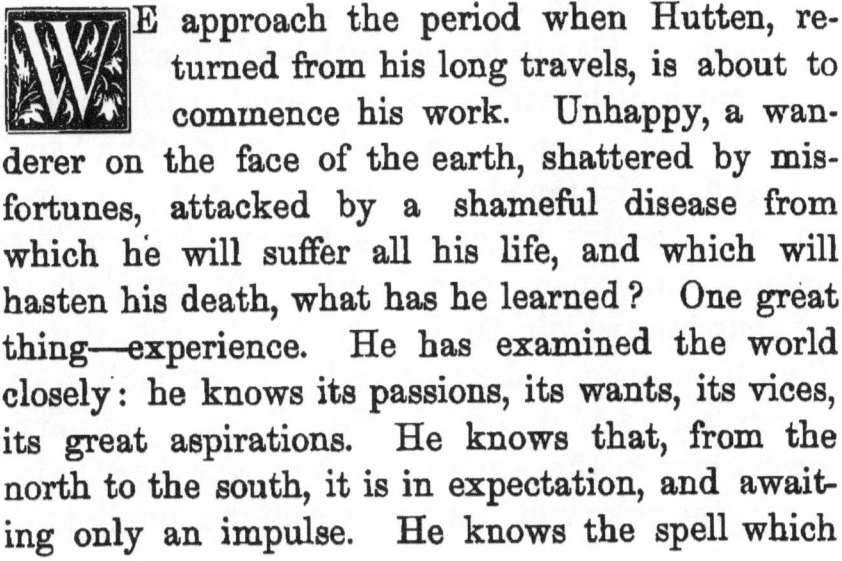E approach the period when Hutten, returned from his long travels, is about to commence his work.   Unhappy, a wanderer on the face of the earth, shattered by misfortunes, attacked by a shameful disease from which he will suffer all his life, and which will hasten his death, what has he learned ?   One great thing—experience.   He has examined the world closely : he knows its passions, its wants, its vices, its great aspirations.   He knows that, from the north to the south, it is in expectation, and awaiting only an impulse.   He knows the spell which

will arouse it.　He has suffered: he will take part
with those who suffer.　He has studied on the spot
the secrets of the Roman tyranny: he will smite it
to the heart.　At the same time, he has developed
his intellectual capacities: he remains a poet, but
he has become a learned man; he has acquired a
perfect acquaintance with the marvels of Greek
and Latin genius brought to light at the Renaissance.　His verses everywhere make for him ad-
mirers and friends.　Young men set out to listen
to him, on the vague report that he has commenced
a course of instruction.　He occupies one of the
highest positions among the learned men of that
learned century.　And his knowledge is not the
dead knowledge of books and vain formulas; it is
the instrument of liberation.　That spirit of liberty
which had pervaded his character from his infancy, which his earliest struggles had increased in
him, and which had been the most ardent sentiment of his adventurous youth, he brought back
enlarged, enlightened, purified by meditation and
travel.　To this he added a fervent love of his
country, and a passionate faith in the grandeur of
the mission which he had to fill in the world.
Than him, none had more pride of nationality, or
deeper hatred of all foreign rule.　What shocks and
revolts him in the pontifical power, as a free Christian, is the yoke which it imposes on the conscience;

but, at the same time, and chiefly, it is the empire
which it pretends to exercise over Germany.   Thus,
though he neglects not to pierce, with his best
directed and most poignant sarcasms, the unheard-
of corruptions of the Roman court, he may with
good reason be reckoned the representative of the
political aspect of the Reformation, just as Luther
—whom he preceded and encouraged in the struggle
—is the special representative of its religious aspect.

Hutten was of short stature; his body was bent
by disease, and by the hardships of his youth.
But his expressive countenance, his sparkling eyes,
told immediately all the feelings of his soul.   His
enemies were often terrified at the tremendous
energy which appeared in that lofty countenance;
while his friends read in it only the nobleness and
generosity of his intellect and heart.   His character
was exceedingly amiable, without hauteur, without
pretension, full of readiness to oblige, and of kind
attentions to women and children, and for the
humblest of mankind.   During his happiest years,
Budæus (5) praises in him these amiable qualities;
and Zwingle bestows on him the same praise, at the
end of his life, when so many misfortunes and de-
ceptions might well have embittered his spirit.
His wit, nourished by serious studies, enlarged by
an attentive observation of men and things, had an
irresistible charm: it sparkled in refined remarks,

in curious comparisons, in unexpected sallies. All
the learned and distinguished men of his time were
his friends, and remained so. One only—Erasmus (6)—betrayed him in his last hour; but Erasmus, enamoured of a quiet life, betrayed less the
man than the unfortunate.

Such was Hutten, when a tragical event threw
him into the midst of the strifes of his time.

VI.

E learned at the same time the death of
his friend and protector, Eitelwolf von
Stein, and the assassination of his cousin,
Hans von Hutten, by the Duke of Wurtemberg.
To the first he gave a touching and tender regret;
to the second, a memorable vengeance.

The Huttens had rendered important services to
the Duke of Wurtemberg. In a revolt of the peasantry, they had given him the victory by leading the
Franconian nobility to his aid. They believed themselves sure of his friendship, and he made warm
protestations of gratitude. He requested of old
Ludwig von Hutten that he would confide to him
his son, who was accounted the most accomplished
knight of Franconia. He held out the most brilliant

inducements, saying that he wished, in the person of this young man, to requite the obligations which he owed to the family.   The youthful Hutten hesitated long, as if he had had a presentiment of his fate ; but the father thought it his duty not to let slip the opportunity which fortune placed before his son.

The Duke overwhelmed the young knight with favours, and kept him constantly at his side; while the latter gave himself up with delight to the enchantments of that court life, where, by a rare good fortune, he enjoyed at once the friendship of the prince, and the good-will of the nobles and people.   He was soon attached to the country by a closer and softer tie ; he married the daughter of the Marshal of Wurtemberg.

After some months of unmingled happiness, he learned from his wife herself that she was beloved by the Duke.   That information struck him like a thunderbolt.   He rushed to the presence of the Duke, with the agony of outraged friendship, rather than with the resentment of an injured husband. He reproached him with his passion, and entreated him to combat it ; but the Duke, in the delirium of desire, threw himself at his feet, and did not blush to ask him to sanction his love for his wife, permitting him in return to aspire to the favours of the Duchess.   The young noble repulsed with contempt this infamous bargain.   From that time his resolution was taken to quit the court, and to withdraw his wife from attempts, in which, as yet, he did not know her complicity.

After long delays, caused by the opposition of the Duke, his departure was fixed, when he was invited to a farewell hunting party. He joined the Duke without mistrust, and without arms. The Duke was armed. He gave the young man a most flattering reception, and attached him to his side in order to converse with him more familiarly. They soon became separated from the rest of the court; and upon arriving in the heart of the forest, where two horses could not ride abreast, the Duke made the unhappy young man go before him. Suddenly he threw himself upon him from behind, and ran him through the body with his sword, not ceasing from his murderous attack until he had given him seven mortal wounds. Then—adding cowardly outrage to crime—he loosed the belt of the dead man, fastened it round his neck, and hung him up to a tree. On regaining his escort with haggard eyes and blood-stained hands, he informed them that, in virtue of his right as a free judge, he had taken vengeance on an adulterer!

The fatal news spread rapidly through Germany, and roused a universal feeling of horror. Everywhere the Duke met indignation and contempt; but, as if he believed himself above punishment, he paraded his crime, and lived publicly with the wife of his victim (7).

————◆————

VII.

HUTTEN was at the baths of Ems when he learned from a friend this frightful crime. His first feeling was grief, and sympathy with the bereaved father; but he determined not to shed useless tears, and resolved to pursue the criminal until punishment should overtake him.

With this view he hastened to reconcile himself with his father, and then took up the cause of the family. Letters, poems, orations, were in turns employed by him to rouse Germany against the tyrant. He fulminated against him five harangues, five philippics full of wrath and vigour. He imparted to Latin, to that dead language, all the life of his ardent soul. He does not disguise the passion which animates him; he gives himself up to all its vehemence, and all its coarseness. He demands of the princes the judgment and punishment of the criminal, and does not conceal from them, that if they refuse, the Huttens will know right well how to do justice to themselves.

' Know, princes' (he exclaims), 'what will be thought of you if you abandon our cause. The whole German people will be animated with a just indignation : they will curse your pride, your hardness of heart; they will deem you accomplices in the crime which you have neglected to punish. Your honour is at stake; reflect well on this. They will say that this man is your peer—this man, who ought to be placed beyond the pale of human communion. Let justice do her office, and do not constrain us to have recourse to force. As to myself, nothing shall make me endure such an injury : I shall renounce only with life the pursuit of that great criminal. These are the feelings of all my kindred ; and how many others share in them ! If you abandon us, it will only remain to take up arms; and then what will become of Germany ? At least she will know that we are not to blame for these misfortunes, that we have done everything to obtain justice, and that we have given the signal of war in spite of ourselves, and constrained by your desertion.'

In these orations Hutten appeared as the avenger of an outraged family ; and, as has been said of him, he prosecuted a true *vendetta*. But these orations have a still greater importance in his life : they revealed to Germany, and perhaps to himself, the politician, as well as the great writer. Hutten made a national cause of his own private wrong, and raised it to the importance of an affair of state.

At the outset, he recalls the services which the Huttens have rendered to the Duke of Wurtemberg; and here is how he treats that first revolt of the Swabian peasantry:—

'A conspiracy had been formed against him. The peasantry could no longer support his tyranny, his imposts, his rapacity, his extortions of every description! How would Germany have been convulsed! What perils, princes, would have menaced you, through the fault of a single individual, if that contagion had been allowed to spread! For, although at first their demands were but too just, evil counsellors crept in among them, and corrupted their original designs. All the scoundrels enlisted in their ranks, and thenceforward there was no diversity of opinion about massacring the nobility, plundering the rich, and overthrowing everything. Such was the danger that menaced Germany. The Franconian knights, sent by Ludwig von Hutten, saved Germany: they saved the Duke, but they could not cure the vices which would lead anew to similar convulsions!'

Undoubtedly, this appreciation of the rising of the German peasantry is not that with which history will agree. She will have more sympathy for these poor wretches, who only rose against an intolerable yoke, and fought valiantly around the iron-shod shoe (Bundschuh), which served them

for a standard.   But she will not deny that acts of
violence and atrocity sullied a cause just in itself;
and, even while taking the part of the ignorant, she
will bow herself before the first impartial judgment
pronounced by a noble upon that great popular
movement.

Hutten afterwards narrates the crime, and demands the punishment of the criminal.   'You owe
it to the honour of your country; you owe it to
yourselves, Swabians.   It is time to throw off the
yoke of that execrable tyrant!   No! believe not
that our knights can attempt to protect that man,
to assist his abominable passions.   We are armed
less against you, than for Germany; and if we had
been able, we would have saved you all.   His violence, his tyranny, are not imputable to us; they
are the crimes of his own individual wickedness.
And who have suffered from them more than we
have?   His impunity has encouraged him in fresh
crimes.   He believes that he may do anything: he
has confiscated your goods, destroyed your houses,
killed your best citizens.   There is a great reason
for inflicting upon him an exemplary punishment.
Germany knows but too well what would be the
results of his impunity!'

To these orations Hutten added a dialogue,
entitled *Phalarismus*.   It is the meeting of Phalaris
and the Duke of Wurtemberg in hell.   Phalaris

congratulates himself on seeing a man his equal in cruelty. He gives him, however, some good lessons in tyranny :—

'Above all, liberate your soul from the fear of God, and from every feeling of humanity. The better and more virtuous a man is, the more you will suspect him as an enemy, and will hasten to get rid of him : in this way you will make yourself feared. At the same time, you will take care to attach some followers by your generosity: they will chant your praises among the people. Be profuse to them, without thinking of counting the money which you have taken from the rest. One great thing is to have good spies, who will bring you an exact account of what is said, thought, and done. Whatever you may do, arrange it so as to give a creditable appearance to your acts; so that, if they do not see you do good, they may at least have no certain proof that you do evil. Often, you must even do something just, noble, and courageous. There is one great point: do not forget it. A single good action, well proved, will efface the remembrance of many crimes. In particular, direct all the penetration of your intellect to discern those whom you ought to fear, and those whom you can seduce. And if, in spite of all, you find yourself in some great danger, there remains to you a last resort, often attempted in Germany, never well executed: gain over the populace by summoning them to the destruction of the rich. As to your pleasures, if you happen to love a woman, and her husband refuses to give her up, get rid of the insolent, but secretly. Such are the rules of tyranny; if that Syracusan had followed them, he would not have fallen from a tyrant to a schoolmaster.'

These writings made an immense impression in Germany. The Emperor, however, hesitated to punish a prince; and it was not until 1519 that vengeance overtook the criminal. Put to the ban of the Empire, he was hunted from Wurtemberg by the indignant people, assisted by an army which Franz von Sickingen (8) commanded, and in which Hutten served. It was in this campaign that the friendship of these two knights commenced.

I do not intend to follow the details of that war; but I must specially mention one event, connected with it, which had an incalculable influence upon the life of Hutten. He had made himself master of the political affairs of Germany; he had studied, to assist his vengeance, all their springs. His voice had made itself heard beyond the little circle of philosophers who, up to that time, had alone appreciated its power: it had gone forth to the people, and re-echoed through the whole nation. His name was associated in the popular imagination with the sad story which affected him so strongly: he had his place in the tragedy.   At the same time, he had viewed princes close at hand : he knew their ambitions, their cabals, and how the Emperor, the venerated representative of national unity, had in reality but little power.   He understood one of the evils of Germany.   He had had a glimpse of the other in his travels, and soon he will study it better at Rome herself.   But, previously, he will fight his first great battle against religious fanaticism, and obtain one of his most brilliant triumphs.

VIII.

THE natural opposition of the Scholastics and the Humanists could not fail to result in an open war.   In truth, the question at issue between them, related to nothing of less importance than the empire over the souls of men, the direction of their intellects, the substitution of a new moral world for that which was old and worn out.   That final strife, however, burst forth in an unexpected manner ; for when questions have been mentally decided, the most trivial incident rouses them, with intense force, into action.

One of the most moderate and timid among the adherents of the new method gave the signal for that memorable combat. John Reuchlin (9) was a learned man, rather than an original or sympathetic intellect : his spirit lacked boldness ; his style, warmth and brilliancy ; but he possessed the passion for learning in the highest degree. Wherever there were any crumbs fallen from the table of the masters to be picked up—to use his own words— there he hastened to proceed. At Paris, in the Vatican, at Florence, and at Basle, he had reaped an ample harvest ; and he hastened to call the world to partake with him. He did incontestable service to the cause of Latin literature by the publication of a dictionary, and to that of Greece by the publication of a small grammar. He spared neither trouble nor money to procure editions of the ancient authors, either in MS., or as they were issued from the printing-presses of Italy. He was the first German who possessed a complete edition of Homer. But his insatiable curiosity did not confine itself to classical antiquity : he turned his attention also to the study of Hebrew. ' No one before me ' (he affirms with legitimate pride) ' had known how to combine in a single volume the grammatical rules of the Hebrew language ; and, in despite of envy, I am and remain the first. *Exegi monumentum ære perennius.*' With a view of

improving himself in this study, he had become
intimate with several rabbis, by whom he was
initiated into the mysteries of the Kabbala.   But
it was not from that quarter that the storm arose
which disturbed him in his learned labours.

Pfefferkorn, a converted Jew, had published a
book, in which, with the fanaticism of a neophyte,
he accused his ancient co-religionists of adoring the
sun and moon, and of insulting Christianity in the
most odious manner.   That book was welcomed as
a special piece of good fortune by the theologians
of Cologne, and especially by Hochstraten, Prior of
the Dominicans, and Inquisitor for the three ecclesiastical electorates.   They represented the Jewish
books as dangerous and heretical, and demanded of
the Emperor an order to burn them.   Maximilian
had no objection to this literary *auto da fè*; but his
councillors, many of whom belonged to the modern
school, and who all detested the Inquisition, considered it advisable to consult the Faculties of
Theology, and the most learned men in Hebrew
literature.   The theologians of Cologne had no
hesitation in ranging themselves on the side of
Hochstraten.   They drew up a memorial, in which
they endeavoured to establish, with much show of
learning, the startling proposition that the Jews
were heretics, and that, as such, it was the
Emperor's right and duty to punish them.   The

Faculties of Paris, Erfurth, Louvain, and Mayence, were, as might be expected, of the same opinion; but Reuchlin adopted the opposite view of the question, and all independent and enlightened men were of his opinion.

He had been consulted by the Archbishop of Mayence, and had answered with remarkable moderation. He pointed out that many Jewish books could not but be very useful to Christianity; that the greater number took no notice of it; and that, consequently, if it was absolutely necessary to burn, a selection, at least, should be made. That moderation was a crime in the eyes of the fanatics. The memorial of Reuchlin, destined for the eyes of the Archbishop of Mayence alone, was, in some unknown manner, communicated to Pfefferkorn, and to the theologians of Cologne. They attacked it immediately with the utmost violence. Reuchlin replied. His answer was burned. He published a second, and was forthwith cited to appear before the Inquisition.

The moment was decisive. It was essential for the Dominicans to strengthen their authority, always disputed, and definitively to establish the Inquisition in the heart of that German land which repulsed it with horror. For the innovators, it was equally essential to conquer liberty and safety.

It was then a war to the death, and every one

felt it to be so. The established authorities did all in their power to prevent a strife which might draw all into its vortex. The Inquisition having assembled at Mayence in 1513, the Archbishop ordered it to dissolve. The Pope remitted the affair to the Bishop of Spire, who condemned the accusers of Reuchlin.

But the theologians did not account themselves vanquished. They burned anew the writings of Reuchlin. The foreign Faculties also did so, especially that of Paris, although public opinion in France was loud against that excess of intolerance. Fortified by such support, Hochstraten turned to the Pope, and set out for Rome, accompanied by a numerous suite, and furnished with a large sum of money, there to plead the cause of the old theology against the Humanists. The Pope was greatly embarrassed. How could he acquit Reuchlin without injuring those powerful Universities, true pillars of the church, and those religious orders, whose assistance was so necessary for the sale of indulgences? And how condemn him, without raising a storm, whose results no one could foresee? He suspended the cause; but, in reality, the Humanists had conquered.

· IX.

UTTEN celebrated the victory even before it had been achieved, so confident was he in the strength of the new school.

The *Triumphus Capnionis* — Capnio was the learned name of Reuchlin—is one of the most remarkable of Hutten's writings. After the eulogy of the victor, as in ancient triumphs, he makes for him a train of vanquished foes. He is full of wild energy. He depicts in glowing colours the corruption of the enemies of all truth, of all liberty, their ignorance, their superstition, their barbarism. He paints their portraits ; as, for example, that of the Inquisitor, Hochstraten :—

'Are God or religion spoken of? On a sudden he cries out, To the fire ! to the fire ! Does one write some book? To the fire with the book and the author! Do you speak truth ? To the fire ! Do you utter falsehood? To the fire ! Do you act justly ? To the fire ! Do you commit injustice ? To the fire ! He is all over fire : he breathes fire ; he lives on fire ! To the fire ! to the fire ! such is his first and his last word.'

In this poem the satire does not smile. It is the first cry of an indignant conscience. It is violent, even brutal. Later, Hutten will be more measured

in the form of his writings, but not less cutting;
he will avail himself of the nimble weapon of
ridicule. On this occasion he is armed with
the lash and the mace, and crushes and over-
whelms his antagonists. Let us mark well this
first appearance of Hutten upon the field of battle,
which he will leave no more. Here is his procla-
mation :—

'Gird up your loins, Theologians, and take to
flight. More than twenty of us have conspired for
your exposure and ruin. We owe it to the innocence of Capnio, to your own wickedness, to the
republic of letters. We owe it to the religion
which you have wrapped in darkness, and on
which we have poured the light. Jerome has re-
appeared : the Gospel has seen the day. A number of Greek and Latin authors have been published. Everywhere there is ardent working ; and
you, what do you do ? By what right do you
usurp the title of theologians, you who have reduced that noble science to a repetition of vain
prating, of sterile and verbose follies and senilities?
You only know how to persecute those to whom
we owe so many wonders. Many are arraying their
ranks to oppose you. I enter the first into the
lists, not because I am the most skilful, but because
I am the most eager. Come on, then, conspirators,
to the work ! to the work ! Our chains are broken !

The die is cast![1] To fall back is impossible! No!
the Turks are not more odious than these men!
But Germany has now her eyes opened; the veil
has fallen; she sees you at full length! You have
reigned too long, owing to some fatal destiny, or
to the crimes of those who have endured it. What
Pope so unjust as to impose that yoke upon us!
and what Emperor so cowardly as to submit to it!
But you have conspired against Capnio in good
time. Germany could no longer remain under an
illusion when she saw you attack such a man. She
felt that her honour had been made sport of! She
has raised herself as one man to defend it! Re-
joice then with me, fellow-countrymen; but let
that victory, so hard to win, learn you at the same
time where your forbearance should stop!'

X.

ALMOST at the same time as the Triumph
of Capnio, appeared that powerful satire,
known as '*Epistolæ Obscurorum virorum,*'
which struck so deadly a blow at monastic estab-
lishments and at the Papacy. The plot is very

---

[1] This is the first time that I meet with the expression, which will
afterwards become the motto of Hutten.

simple : they are letters, supposed to be written
chiefly by monks and theologians—but a few by
jurists and doctors—to Ortuinus Gratus, who, along
with Hochstraten and Tunger (10), stood at the head
of the persecutors of Reuchlin.   Written in the bad
Latin which at that time was the usual language
of the monks, these letters display the peculiar
phraseology and vulgarisms characteristic of the
last representatives of Scholasticism.   They unveil,
with a simplicity full of tact and cleverness, the
secret history of the mendicant orders, their vices,
their hatred of all serious instruction, their ignorance,
their plots against Reuchlin and the Humanists.
'That composition' (says Herder, cited by a biographer of Hutten) 'strikes so truly, depicts so
faithfully, Pfefferkorn and Ortuinus, and all their
spawn, that we find them there just as God had
made them.   It is a national satire, full of fire, wit,
and a marvellous exactitude of detail.   Do not object, fastidious critics, to the name of pamphlet;
all true and lively satire is a pamphlet.   The more
a pamphlet is general, and at the same time telling,
the more it is worth.   And the pamphlet in question
struck far and truly.   The lukewarm satire,
which is neither fish nor flesh, has never done any
good.   Hutten's satire has been very useful, and
why? It was entirely true.   It had life and truth,
like all that he has ever written.' (11.)

And, in reality, the great excellence of this book is its truth,—so much so, that those whom it overwhelmed with ridicule, took it at first for a serious production. 'It is interesting to observe,' writes Sir Thomas More to Erasmus, 'how much the *Epistolæ Obscurorum virorum* please both the learned and unlearned. When the latter see us laughing at them, they fancy that we laugh only at the style, which they do not attempt to defend; but under that somewhat barbarous language, say they, what an abundance of excellent maxims! It is a pity that the book has not another title: it would take a hundred years before these imbeciles would comprehend to what an extent they have been taken in.' Erasmus also relates that, in Brabant, a Dominican prior bought a great many copies of the work, to present to his superiors, under the belief that it had been written in praise of their order! (12.) Behold the Atlases who believe themselves destined to uphold a falling church!'

This satire, the most perfect specimen of that species of writing in the German language, recalls in more than one point our immortal *Ménippée*. It recalls to memory the great name of Voltaire. Like the work of that able man, it has spirit, vivacity, occasionally too great liberty of language, cutting and relentless personality; and, lastly, a wit which hides all. Its ridicule springs from the

same source; it usually attacks the same objects,
the histories of apocryphal saints and of imaginary
relics. It ridicules, for example, as Voltaire has
somewhere done, I believe, the legend of these
three kings of Cologne, who were, perhaps, three
Westphalian peasants. Finally, it delights to seek
in the Scriptures themselves its keenest shafts; and
the history of Ezekiel, certain too practical maxims
of Ecclesiastes, and certain crudities of the pro-
phets, without doubt symbolical, are found in it as
in a jest-book.

It is in the nature of such a work to be un-
translatable. I prefer to send my readers to the
book itself, rather than attempt an impossible rendering (13). On this occasion, however, irony, in
the service of common sense, conquered. The mendicant orders, and the old scholastic framework, of
which they were the firmest bulwarks, have never
recovered it.

The German monks were not deceived, like those
of England and Brabant. They begged, or they
bought, from the Pope a Bull, which ordered the
burning of the book and its authors, *when they should
be discovered;* for the pamphlet had appeared anony-
mously. It was sometimes claimed for Erasmus,
sometimes for Reuchlin; but from its first appearance, friends and enemies agreed in recognising, in
the greater part of it, the hand which had written

the *Triumphus Capnionis*, and modern criticism has placed this fact beyond doubt (14).

We may suppose that the judgment of the Pope was less galling to the authors than that of Erasmus. As long as the letters were in manuscript, no one had more keenly enjoyed them; he had learned several of them by heart; he recited them to his friends; he sent them as wonders to his illustrious correspondents in France and England. When they were published, however, and the tempest burst, he feared to be taken for the author; and lost no time in writing that these letters were very disagreeable to him—that he appreciated their cutting irony, but that he abhorred all personalities (15).

Hutten could console himself for this cowardly desertion in contemplating the success of his work. The war had opened by a victory : that first success was, for him, an omen and an encouragement.

After that first battle, the strife was waged beyond the head of Reuchlin; he almost disappeared in the smoke of the combat. However, we must relate the termination of this first episode. In 1520, after the brilliancy thrown on the scene by the writings of Hutten and Luther, the Dominicans at length obtained the condemnation of Reuchlin. But times were greatly changed; Germany no longer gave any weight to a sentence which, but lately, would have led the condemned to the stake. Only, Franz von Sickingen, the protector of all the oppressed, and the friend of Hutten, took up the cause of Reuchlin, and struck such terror into the Dominicans, that they hastened to promise never to molest the protégé of the brave knight. Reuchlin died the same year.

———◆———

XI.

WHAT sadder lot than to be disowned by his relations, by those even to whom he has sacrificed all, except his faith! It is the last, the bitterest trial, which only the strongest spirits can resist. It was not spared to Hutten.

In his first grief, after the crime which had plunged him into mourning, his family had been reconciled to him, and Hutten rejoiced in the reconciliation. But he was far from receiving the welcome which he had a right to expect after so long an absence, after so many misfortunes. They did not disguise the contempt which they entertained for those studies which were his honour and delight. What had he learned? Nothing. What was he? A learned man, a poet, a being useless, almost a disgrace to his relations. 'One day,' says he, jestingly, 'a noble friend of the family asking

D

of one of my relations by what title he should address me : "Alas," was the answer, "he is still
nothing."' But if he had consented to enter the
convent! It was not that his father was in reality
much chagrined that he had disobeyed him in that
particular ; he confessed one day to Crotus Rubianus, with a mixture of regret and paternal self-
love, that he did not believe that his son was fitted
for such a life. But, as a provident father, he
wished that he should be something, and Hutten
was nothing, not even Doctor. ' He must be
Doctor, or at least Master or Bachelor of Laws,
or else he is nothing. They don't ask what a man
is really worth, but what he is. Fortune, title, are
everything ; virtue, nothing.'

Three high roads then conducted to a position
in the world—war, the convent, the law. War?
In spite of his incontestable bravery, Hutten was
unfitted for it, since he was a learned mau. His
relations and his friends regarded with contempt his
limbs distorted by disease and enfeebled by study,
his forehead wrinkled by thought, his hands fitter for
the pen than the sword.—The convent? Nothing
could overcome the horror with which Hutten had
regarded it even at that age when everything appears gay and bright.—There remained but the law.
The doctors of civil law made a very good figure in
sixteenth century society. They peopled the courts

of princes and of the Emperor. 'They fill like
sponges the ears of the great; they are their advisers, their agents in all affairs of peace or war.
It matters little whether they are indoctrinated
with learning, provided they have the title of
Doctor; with that title, they are sure of being
everywhere well received. The princes ruin themselves to enrich them.' To sum up all, to be
Doctor of Laws was no derogation of nobility, even
in a noble Franconian; and it was therefore decided that Hutten should repair to Italy to acquire
that precious title.

He set out on his journey with great repugnance; for he would have preferred proceeding to
Basle to be near Erasmus, to continue under that
illustrious master his favourite Greek and Latin
studies. However, he was determined to satisfy
the desires of his parents, and he applied himself
to study with conscientious ardour. But he was
not captivated by the science of the Bartholists, by
that vain and unproductive learning which the last
commentators had established in the schools, and
which held the ascendant until driven forth by
Cujas and Donneau. The more he studied it,
the more he detested that false science, which
pretended to imprison in antiquated formulas, to
deaden and to petrify the law, which, rightly
understood, lends animation and security to social

life. And by a contradiction more apparent than
real, with the very spirit of the Renaissance, he
attached himself with a thoughtful ardour to the
last vestiges of the national law. He did so because, in his opinion, antiquity was not a model
which the modern world ought servilely to copy :
what he sought for in her, was the sacred fire which
might re-illumine the torch of life. 'How much
more happy was Germany' (he exclaims in his
preface to '*Nemo*'[1]) 'before the invasion of these
Bartholists, who have come, with their innumerable
volumes, to take the place of the time-honoured
customs of our forefathers! What cities are better
governed than those which have shut their gates
against them! Look at the Saxons on the shores
of the Baltic : how speedy and impartial is justice
among them! They only look to their customs,
while we drag on our law-suits for twenty years,
led on by the contradictory opinions of six and
thirty doctors. How can we form a favourable
opinion of their science, when all their books do
not teach them to administer law in a uniform
manner ?'

[1] That preface, under the form of a letter to Crotus Rubianus, defends the cause of the Humanists against the Bartholists and the
theologians. It is one of the most important documents connected
with the history of the Renaissance. With regard to the poem to
which it serves as an introduction, it is a long string of puns, sometimes ingenious, but without any special interest.

But the most important result of Hutten's journey to Italy was, that he saw upon the spot, in Rome herself, the corruption of the church. All those who have seen papal Rome in her palmy days, convey substantially the same impression. Boccaccio, Hutten, Luther, Montaigne, Rabelais, differ only in the expression of their disgust. The Papacy, which fancied that it had burned the last heretic in Huss, and which, after the fruitless attempts at Basle and at Constance, feared no longer a general council, which she was besides determined never again to convoke, gave herself up, without restraint, without fear, to all sorts of excesses. After the bloody and scandalous reign of the Borgias, came the warlike sway of Julius II., under which were to be seen Italians fighting Italians, and a Pope pointing his cannon against Christians, in order to realize the projects of a detestable ambition. Assassinations, debauchery, the most shameful vices, the most unbridled luxury, courtesans, and a swarm of infamous men around the princes of the Church—idleness, ignorance, bad faith, perjury, in the relations of public and private life—make up the picture which historians and travellers have painted of the court of Rome. And in order to defray these unlimited expenses, money was drawn, or rather extorted, from Christendom, under the pretence of a war, constantly adjourned, against the Turks, or in order to complete the always unfinished Church of St Peter; all ecclesiastical dignities were put up for sale; annats were rendered more frequent by the systematic nomination of old men to benefices; the price of the *pallium* was raised, and that infamous traffic in indulgences extended, where heaven was put up to sale, and all crimes, even the most infamous and nameless ones, pardoned for money. Germany, which has ever possessed in a very high degree the religious sentiment, was the worst treated of all countries, and the most exhausted by the drain of continual subsidies. Hutten was indignant at seeing the contempt with which the Italians regarded the country of the Othos and the Fredericks. He returned home, swearing in his heart an eternal hatred and a ceaseless war against the papal tyranny and corruption.

His residence in Italy was marked by two incidents which procured him great honour in Germany. One day, in the neighbourhood of Viterbo, he heard five Frenchmen scoffing at the Emperor Maximilian. He interfered to defend his sovereign. The discussion grew warm; insults first, and then blows, were exchanged. Swords were drawn. The five Frenchmen at once threw themselves upon Hutten, who, placing his back to a wall, sustained their attacks, killed one of his as-

sailants, and put the others to flight (16).   Forced
to leave Rome in order to escape from their vengeance, he repaired to Bologna.   At that town a
quarrel took place between the German and Italian
students.   The matter was brought before the
Podestà, and Hutten, who acted as advocate for
his countrymen, spoke with such warmth, that the
judge wished to throw him into prison.

He was therefore obliged to quit Italy without
having obtained the title of Doctor.   But instead,
the Emperor Maximilian—whom Hutten's exploits
were exactly calculated to please—knighted him,
and bestowed upon him the title of Imperial Poet
and Orator (17).   The laurel crown had been
woven, and was placed upon his head, in April
1517, by the Pearl of Augsburg, the beautiful
Constance, the daughter of Peutinger (18).

XII.

UPON seeing his son crowned Imperial Poet
and Orator, Hutten's father thought that
he was at length something, and con-
soled himself for his return without the title of
Doctor of Laws.   He received him with great kind-
ness at his castle of Steckelberg, where Hutten

remained for some time, uncertain as to his future
course of life, and undecided whether he should
establish himself near the Emperor, or with his
ancient protector, the Archbishop of Mayence.

His leisure was not, however, lost to the cause
to which he had devoted his life. In December
1517, he issued his declaration of war against the
Pope, and commenced the campaign by the publication of the book of Laurentius Valla (19) upon the
donation of Constantine. This work, like several
of the writings of Hutten, was printed at the
castle of Steckelberg; for these champions of
liberty did not separate themselves from that powerful weapon in the armoury of freedom, with which
the genius of Guttenberg had provided them!

The donation of Constantine—that audacious
imposture, upon which are founded the temporal
sovereignty of the Pope, and his pretensions to
secular dominion over the whole of the West—is
now judged. Roman Catholic authors themselves
no longer defend it: as in the case of the false
Decretals, they have been forced to acknowledge
that it is apocryphal, and to fall back upon a tradi-
tion, which would only be legitimate if the sources
from which it flows were so themselves. But, in
the fifteenth century, criticism had not yet done its
work, and the Papacy had given up none of the pretensions which it believed it possible to support.

Laurentius Valla shows, with an affluence of learning which now makes us smile, that Constantine
had not given a world to the Holy See ; that even
if he had given it, the donation would have been
null, the Emperor having no right to dismember
the Empire, and the Pope—the Vicar of Him whose
kingdom is not of this world—being still less entitled to receive kingdoms ; and that, finally, even
supposing the donation conferred, and valid, it
would have lapsed, the Popes having rendered
themselves unworthy of their rights by their detestable tyranny.   'I shall say it; for, strong in
the support of God, I fear not men.   No, I have
not seen a single Pope who dreamed of the happiness of the people, or who even ruled well.   Who
is it, if not the Pope, who sows war among peaceful
nations ?   He is greedy of the riches of others,
prodigal of his own.   He makes a traffic not only
of the state, but of the church herself, and of the
Holy Spirit.   He would recover, he says, from the
wrongful possessors the donation conferred by
Constantine !   Eh ! what matters it to the church ?
When the Pope shall possess all these territories,
will the church be less dishonoured and disturbed
by so many crimes, by luxury, by furious passions ?
The Pope gives the excuse and the example for all
these infamies.   We may say to him, with St Paul
and Isaiah, " Thou therefore which teachest an-

other, teachest thou not thyself? Thou that preachest a man should not steal, dost thou steal? Thou that sayest a man should not commit adultery, dost thou commit adultery? Thou that abhorrest idols, dost thou commit sacrilege? Thou that makest thy boast of the law, through breaking the law dishonourest thou God? For the name of God is blasphemed among the Gentiles through you." May I live to see the day when the Pope shall be no longer the Vicar of Cæsar, but of Jesus Christ; when we shall no longer hear of that horrible spectacle—Christians making war against the church, and the church attacking Perugia and Bologna. No! it is not the church that makes war against the faithful; it is the Pope! Then the Pope will be, in truth, the holy father of all the nations: far from stirring up war among Christians, from the height of his pontifical throne, he will appease the discords which others have excited!'

Such, speaking generally, is the part which the Ultramontanists of our times have assigned to the Papacy of the Middle Ages, but which history has never seen her fulfil. The undaunted writer who wrote these noble words was condemned, it is almost needless to say. His book was everywhere hunted out and burned, and had fallen into almost complete oblivion, when Hutten found it in the library of the Abbey of Fulda. The moment was well chosen to give fullest effect to such a work. Luther, after having commenced the war against indulgences, was troubled in conscience, and hesitated to attack the Pope. The spirits of all were on the stretch, awaiting the event; for a nameless instinct warned them that the hour was come.

By a master-stroke of audacity, which insured him impunity, Hutten dedicated the book to the Pope himself, to Leo X.

'Although' (he says) 'all your predecessors have condemned the discourse of Laurentius Valla, because it impugns the donation of Constantine, I dedicate it to you with confidence. I have no fear, as some think, that you will be offended at my offering. Since your elevation to the Holy See, you are the hope and the love of the world, the restorer of peace, the protector of the arts and sciences. You have silenced the warlike blast of the trumpet of Julius II.; you have promised peace, and consequently also justice, security, and those truly royal virtues, mildness and clemency. My dedication will furnish a testimony to succeeding ages, that, under your pontificate, men might think and speak freely, might utter and write the truth.

'The work of Laurentius Valla undoubtedly accuses your predecessors; but it is even that which makes it so useful, because it attacks the enemies of the human race. What other name, indeed, can we give to those Popes who engross the treasures of every country, and impose upon all nations the most crushing of yokes; who despoil kings of their thrones, and private persons of their property? Can we call those men Vicars of Christ who have done nothing which Christ has done and commanded? No! they deserve rather the name of thieves and tyrants! They have made a traffic of grace, of temporal and spiritual dispensations. They have derived a revenue from the sins of other men, and from their punishment even after death; and, every year, they have extorted from Christians their last penny, under the pretext of a war, which they have never waged, against the Turks, of a temple—that of St Peter—which they have never finished! And in spite of all these things, they would have us to call them, Most Holy Fathers! And if any one permitted himself the slightest criticism on their acts or customs, they at once fired up, and condemned not merely his body, but also his soul. To compare you to such men, would be to offer you a gross insult. And therefore I persuade myself, that you will receive this my offering with pleasure. If you deign to manifest your satisfaction at my exertions, I shall strive to offer you, at some future period, another present of the same description.'

All Hutten's contemporaries speak of the strong impression produced by this bold and well-timed publication. But what testimony can be so valuable as Luther's? 'I have in my hands' (he writes to a friend) 'the donation of Constantine, refuted by Laurentius Valla, and edited by Hutten. Good God! what ignorance, or what perversity in that court of Rome! And how ought we to admire the designs of God, who has allowed falsehoods so impure, shameful, and impudent, to prevail during ages, and be received even into the Decretals, and among the articles of faith, that nothing might be wanting to the most monstrous of monstrosities. I am so agitated, that I scarcely any longer doubt that the Pope is Antichrist. All agrees: what he does, what he says, and what he decrees' (20).

XIII.

AFTER this thunderbolt, the Archbishop of Mayence lost no time in attaching Hutten to himself. This prelate, as we know, was not favourable to the Pope: he too had seen on the spot the corruption of Rome; he had been the victim of her rapacity. His *pallium* had cost him no less than 20,000 florins. Thus he

was not displeased at an attack made on the
Papacy from this side. He changed his views,
however, when he saw that the struggle tended to
nothing less than the complete liberation of lay-
men from the priestly yoke, to the secularization
of the ecclesiastical principalities ; and that, after
the overthrow of the Pope, it would be the turn of
the bishops to tremble for their temporal power.
Hutten did not spare him that shock ; but at this
time he did not yet foresee the ultimate tendency
of the movement. As to Luther, the Archbishop
of Mayence was always his enemy ; the first blow
struck by Luther having injured his interests.
For, as we know, the Pope had authorized the
Archbishop to appropriate the product of the sale
of indulgences within his diocese, in order to reim-
burse him for the extortion of which he had been
the victim at Rome.

Hutten made a journey to Paris on some business
of the Archbishop. There he met those liberal-
minded men, Lefebvre d'Etaples (21), Budée, Copp
(22), and Rueil, and acquired their friendship. He
engaged them in the war which he had undertaken
against the barbarous Scholasticism, or rather he
strengthened them in their hostility to it ; for,
long before, these noble spirits had been enlisted
in the cause.

The ruling thought of Hutten at this period, is

to form a holy league of those who contended for
the freedom of thought against the tyrants of the
human intellect. 'Would to God' (writes he to the
Count Nuenar (23) in 1517) 'that all those were con-
founded who oppose themselves to the revival of
letters, and who would fain trample under foot the
young nursery of all the virtues. As for you, remain true to yourself, and to your design. Be
assured that I shall share in all your labours and
all your perils. I shall spare nothing to gain over
to our cause all those who can be useful to it.
Already, many men of influence are ranged on our
side. The quarrels, also, which are springing up
among the enemies of the truth, and of the true
religion, will hasten their destruction. Perhaps
you know that but lately, at Wittemberg, one
party has protested against indulgences, while
another vindicates them with energy. The chiefs
of both parties are monks : they harangue, they
quarrel with all their might. They print propositions, conclusions, articles. Truly, I hope that
they will destroy each other. The other day, I
said to a monk who related to me these disputes,
" Go on, cease not to destroy each other, that you
also may be destroyed !" If Germany would listen
to me, she would rid herself of that cankering
plague before dreaming of attacking the Turks,
although that also may be very necessary ; for

with the Turks, after all, we only dispute about the Empire, while we endure among ourselves the destroyers of science, manners, and religion !' '

It is remarkable with what disdain Hutten speaks in this letter of the act which commenced the Reformation. At a distance, it seems as if this act had, even at the moment, made the world tremble. It cannot be believed that Germany remained indifferent to it : history has preserved the remembrance of the profound emotion with which that country was affected. But, at that first moment, the enemy of the mendicant orders, the friend of a prince who sold indulgences, was quite headstrong in his friendship and his hatred, and could not disengage his judgment from the influence of the position in which he was placed. Besides, to be correct, it must be added, that at that time the struggle was confined within narrow limits. Many years elapsed before Luther took a decisive step against the Pope, and the writings of Hutten had a considerable influence in the development of his opinions. We have already seen how he had been moved by the work of Laurentius Valla, and we shall again observe, more than once, traces of a similar impression. It is an essential part of the biography of Hutten : by the influence which he exercised upon so original a genius, we may calculate that which he had with the nation.

Before Luther had declared against the Pope, Hutten had already opened the campaign, and produced considerable changes. From 1519, Tetzel dares no longer show himself in public. About the same period, or later, the princes hostile to Luther, the ecclesiastical princes themselves, agree *that they can no longer support the exactions and the iniquities of Rome, and that it is necessary to reassert the ancient liberty.* In their complaints, they display the spirit, and employ the very phrases of Hutten. And thus, side by side with the doctrinal question, about which he was less concerned, Hutten prosecuted the war upon the practical basis of the liberation of the intellect, by the overthrow of the rapacious and corrupt tyranny of the court of Rome.

XIV.

HUTTEN accompanied the Archbishop of Mayence to the Diet of Augsburg in 1518. The recent conquests of the Ottoman arms gave, on this occasion, a peculiar importance to the eternally recurring question of a tax to maintain a war against the infidels. That tax, so often agreed to, had never served, except to minister to Roman corruption and luxury; and now that

E

it was necessary,—now that the war, so to speak, was inevitable, nay, on the very threshold of Germany,—the estates of the kingdom were unwilling to grant anything. Hutten had insisted, in an energetic and eloquent discourse, upon the necessity of defending Christendom, more seriously menaced than ever. And, at the same time, he had pointed out the true means of doing so : by the church and the clergy furnishing the money, while Germany would give her soldiers and her blood. On that occasion, he had declaimed with his accustomed vigour against the exactions of the Popes. His friends entreated him to suppress that part of his oration; but to this he consented with great unwillingness. 'Germany is no longer Germany' (he writes to Pirckheimer) ; 'the liberty of writing exists no longer. He who seeks the truth, and who speaks it, is disgraced. It is no longer possible to discharge one's duty as an honourable man !' This concession to the fears of his friends weighed upon his mind, and afflicted him with such remorse, that in the following year he printed, at his castle of Steckelberg, the discourse unmutilated (24). 'Who then'—he exclaims in his dedication, *To all the freemen of Germany*—'would wish to stifle our liberty, so that we should no longer be able to rise up against any injustice, any exaction ? Let such a one beware ! Liberty, trodden down, will some day burst forth, and annihilate her oppressors. I say so for their own interest : let them leave a little air and space to German liberty. She is not exacting, and is content with little ; but she will not submit to be chained completely, and led away like a slave ! Rather than submit to that excess of ignominy, she may at last become thoroughly aroused, and, in order to save something, take all.'

Courtly life did not suit the independent spirit of Hutten. At the end of some months, he had penetrated into all its hollowness, and criticised it in a charming dialogue. He remained at court, however, because he thought that he could be more useful there than elsewhere.

' It is necessary for me,' he writes to his friend Pirckheimer, ' to throw myself, for the time at least, into active life. I owe it to my family, to myself, and especially to our well-loved studies. I have my plan ; I do not act rashly. I have a well-defined aim towards which I direct my career, which I seek resolutely to attain ; but I cannot succeed by my own unassisted strength. I shall some day tell you, confidentially, how I hope to find the requisite assistance in this court : it would be imprudent to confide it to a letter. Let it suffice you to know, that it is from a sense of duty that I encounter all the tediousness of this life. If my condition appears changed to you, be assured that

my soul is unchanged: I shall always be the same
Hutten; I shall not be unfaithful to my youth, and
I shall advance, always like myself, in different
paths.   With regard to the designs which I cherish,
the fortune to which I may look forward, though
pretty considerable, is not sufficient to carry them
out.   I must endeavour to make my way at court.
And then, may I not attempt to destroy the prejudices of the nobility against the sciences? If they
saw me given up to learned leisure, they would only
be more confirmed in their opinion, that the sciences
emasculate the soul, and make it cowardly and
effeminate. The time for repose has not arrived (25).
Our party gains ground every day.   The councillors
of the Emperor and of the princes are upon our
side: it is on this account that we term the princes
Mecænases and Augustuses, not because they already merit those illustrious names, but in order to
inspire them with a generous emulation.   Up to the
present time we have had tolerable success: I
know more than one who has declared for us from
fear of disgrace.   I am therefore of opinion that we
should do all to gain their good-will: the Bartholists
and the theologians have set us the example; it is
by this means that they have become so powerful.
I see here a great number of illustrious men. . . . .
Eck combats Carlstadt, my fellow-citizen, a virtuous
theologian; he makes war upon Luther and Eras

mus. Erasmus continues to write. Guglielmus
Budæus, the most learned of French nobles, the
most noble of learned men, is finishing his com-
mentaries upon the *Pandects:* I leapt for joy at
that news. Behold, at the same moment, two Her-
culeses, exterminators of monsters—Erasmus and
Budæus. The one destroys the posterity of Accursius, and extirpates the evil brood of the Bartholists; the other attacks the barbarians who conceal
themselves behind the smoke of theology, and brings
to light the Holy Scriptures. Add to them Faber,
that mighty workman in philosophy, and Copp and
Rueil,—the former Dioscorides, the latter Galen.
Oh age, oh literature! How delightful it is to live
now, although the time for repose be not yet arrived!
Barbarism, thine hour is come: gird up thy loins,
and set out on an eternal exile!'

XV.

I DO not pretend to give an account of all
the works of Hutten. I select those
which exercised the greatest influence
on his era, or which best depict his character and his
designs. The year 1519 was one of the busiest of
his life. At the same time that he publishes his
terrible harangues against the tyrant of Wurtem-

berg, and serves in the army that chases him from
his dominions, he edits an edition of Livy, and
launches against Rome and against her legates
three dialogues, full of spirit, eloquence, and irony.
He publishes, and dedicates to Ferdinand, brother
of Charles V., a work against Pope Gregory VII.,
which he found, like the discourse of Valla, buried
in the dust of the Library of Fulda. He keeps up
a voluminous correspondence with all the illustrious
men of his time. 'More than 2000 letters,' says a
contemporary, 'from kings, princes, lords, bishops,
from every man of note, came to him from Italy,
France, Bohemia, Germany, from all countries,
congratulating him on having commenced the war
against the Romanists, and seeking to engage him
to continue it.'

The moment appeared favourable. The Archbishop of Mayence treated Hutten like a friend;
Erasmus assured him that Ferdinand, brother of
Charles V., took a great interest in him; and Sickingen, the better to ensure the co-operation of that
prince, hastened to offer him his services, which
were contended for by kings. Finally, Charles V.
himself appeared likely to be hostile to the Pope,
who had strained every nerve in favour of Francis
I., his competitor for the Empire, and detested rival.
Hutten judged it to be his duty to make a direct
attack upon the Papacy. He hesitated no longer,

but threw himself into the van, shouting his war-cry,—*Alea jacta est!* He announced his determination to all his friends, and made preparations for striking a grand blow.

His mind appears to have been still further strengthened in this resolution by religious meditation. He displays an ardour of faith which is not observable in his previous writings. 'Though I should be certain,' he says, in the preface of his book against Gregory VII., 'that the Pope would direct against me the thunderbolts of his wrath, I would not for that the less speak out what I know to be truth, lest I should have to exclaim with the repentant prophet, "Woe is me, for I am undone, because I am a man of unclean lips!" Truly we must obey God rather than men, and God commands us to speak the truth: He calls Himself the Truth. Paul writes to his disciple: "Preach the word; be instant in season and out of season; reprove, rebuke, exhort, with all long-suffering and doctrine. For the time will come when they will not endure sound doctrine." Christ also wishes us to proclaim the truth undauntedly, and without fearing men, who can destroy the body, but not the soul. "I am come," says our Saviour, "to send fire upon the earth; and what will I if it be already kindled?" It is then, unquestionably, a meritorious action to bring to light concealed truth; and I shall have my reward for doing so, if not on this earth, at least in that heavenly country where every man will be judged according to his works.'

At this time, Hutten requested his family neither to send him money nor to write to him, in order that they might not be compromised, and involved in the perils which he had resolved to incur. That affectionate care for his relations never left him. On the death of his father, he gave up his inheritance, and maintained alone, and without resources, the terrible struggle in which he was engaged. This second portion of his life is entirely self-abnegation.

It seems probable, however, that, at the last moment, his great heart may have hesitated. The family sentiment, the desire for domestic life, was awakened within him more vividly than ever; and he had fancied in a dream a peaceful domestic existence. 'I have a strong desire for repose,' he writes to his friend Piscator, 'and some day I shall satisfy it. But in order to do so, I must have a wife. You know my disposition: I cannot live alone. I must have some one near me with whom I can unbend from my cares and my toils, with whom I can laugh, play, converse gaily, and forget the bitterness of my soul, the griefs of my heart. Get me a wife, then, dear Frederick; and, that you may know what kind of wife I desire, she must be young, handsome, well educated, and modest; she

must have a competence, though not a fortune :
upon riches I do not much insist.   As to her birth,
the wife of Hutten will always be sufficiently noble.'
But he was never destined to enjoy that happiness
of which he dreamed—repose beside a beloved wife.
He was born for strife ; he fulfilled his destiny, and
found repose in the tomb.

XVI.

'I PREPARE a book,' writes Hutten to his
friend Eoban Hess (26), 'which contains
the strongest and the freest comments
upon the bloodsuckers of Rome.'   That book is
the *Vadiscus*, or *Trias Romana*, published at first
in Latin, and a short time afterwards translated
into German.   In his dedication to the knight
von Rotenhan (27), we read: 'I shall not affirm
that this book is good, for it treats of a detestable subject.   Yet I am, perhaps, in the right
to praise it on account of the truth which it contains, and the freedom with which that truth is
stated.   I have never satisfied myself so completely
as in this work.   Our liberties were fettered by the
Pope, I set them free.   The truth was banished
from our country, I bring her back.'
We must translate the whole of this formidable

pamphlet. 'Never,' as is remarked by a biographer of Hutten,[1] 'have the unheard-of abuses and corruptions of the Church of Rome; her infamies and vices, which descended like a flood upon the whole world; her intolerable exactions, especially practised upon Germany; her insults, which rendered these exactions still more unbearable; the extraordinary patience of princes and nations; and the inevitable necessity of a violent revolution; been represented in more true and lively colours. Whoever would wish to know what the Papacy has dared, what our ancestors have borne, should read this book. No one will lay it down without blessing its author, without being animated with the sentiments which inspired him, without acknowledging that such a state of affairs could be no longer supported, and that it was necessary to change it at all hazards' (28).

The *Trias Romana* is a dialogue, in which the interlocutors are Hutten, and one of his friends, Ehrenhold. Hutten relates to him what a traveller of the name of Vadiscus has told him of the court of Rome. These relations are given under the form of triads, often interrupted by the exclamations of Ehrenhold, and by the reflections which the two friends interchange.

'If I am not entirely mistaken,' says Hutten,

---

[1] C. Meiners. Lebens Beschreibungen, t. iii. Zurich, 1797.

'our nation aspires to liberty. The wisest and
the noblest endure with the greatest difficulty the
exactions of the ignorant and corrupt Romanists,
and the insults which they add to their violence.
Things have arrived at such a point, that they can
no longer be borne. Our princes, met together
at Frankfort, most deeply felt the insult when
Cajetan, one of those Romanists *a latere*, exclaimed,
on seeing a long procession of priests magnificently
apparelled, "What handsome grooms we have there!"
Not less insolent was that Roman to whom I spoke
of the oppression of our country, adding that, out
of regard to their own interests, the Romanists
would do well to employ a little more moderation
and address in their robberies. " The barbarians,"
answered he, " are not worthy of having money;
they do not even deserve that we should give ourselves the trouble to extract from them with address
what they still possess." No nation is so generally
and visibly despised at Rome as the Germans; and
why? Because, owing to an overstrained and ill-
understood piety, we suffer ourselves to be pillaged
by those unworthy Romans, of that which their
haughty ancestors could not take from us by force
of arms. Young and old, men and women, merchants and work-people, priests and courtiers, and,
to say the truth, the very Jews themselves, these
bondmen of every nation, laugh at our folly.'

' But the impudence of the vendors of indulgences and of the legates, has had the result of opening the eyes, even of the people, in many districts of Germany. How indignant, for example, were they at Frankfort against these legates, who sold to thousands of persons the permission to eat butter and milk on fast-days; and yet did not blush to make themselves be served with all sorts of meats, under the flimsy pretext that the fish of Germany made them ill! However, it is still greatly to be lamented that they are unwilling to perceive the crimes of the Romanists, and their impudence. It is, therefore, necessary to exclaim, warn, accuse, and strike, until all understand. I know well that this cannot be done without risk; but what great thing is ever achieved without danger? We must write and speak the truth with Christian confidence; knowing how our Saviour Himself has done so, vigorously and without pity, when He denounced the priests and scribes! Following in His steps, we shall prevail against those who abuse the name of God for their earthly ends, who have put their human commandments in the place of those of Christ, and who know neither how to teach good nor to do it. They have made of the word of God a fable; they adore the creature instead of the Creator; they have entered into the Lord's fold, not as shepherds, but as thieves and spoilers. Let us not cease, then, to unmask them. If we cannot ourselves accomplish this great enterprise, we shall perhaps arouse minds more happily constituted, who shall succeed in awakening Christendom from its lethargy and raising it against its oppressors. Germany could not do a greater service to the whole church, and to Christ Himself, than by at once cutting short all these exactions, and by leaving all these copyists and proto-notaries to die of famine. More dangerous than the Turks, they make a traffic of Christ, of His altars, of His sacraments, of heaven itself. But hear what Vadiscus says :—

' " Three things maintain the renown of Rome : the power of the Pope, relics, and indulgences. Three things are brought from Rome by those who go there : a bad conscience, a spoiled stomach, an empty purse. Three things are not to be found at Rome : conscience, religion, truth. The Romans laugh at three things : the virtue of their ancestors, the Papacy of St Peter, the last judgment. Three things abound at Rome : poison, antiquities, empty places. Three things are entirely wanting : simplicity, moderation, and loyalty. The Romans sell three things publicly : Christ, ecclesiastical dignities, and women. Of three things they have a horror : a general council, church reform, and the progress of enlightenment. Three things may cure

Rome of all her vices: the disappearance of superstition, the suppression of the Romish form of worship, and a revolution of her entire organization. Three things are highly prized at Rome: beautiful women, handsome houses, and papal bulls. Three things are common at Rome: pleasure, luxury, and pride. The poor eat three things: cabbages, onions, and garlic. And the rich? The sweat of the poor, swindled wealth, and the spoils of Christendom. Rome possesses three sorts of citizens: Simon the Magician, Judas Iscariot, and the people of Gomorrah. The cardinals drag three trains behind them: one at their robes; another, a band of thieves, assassins, and ruffians; the third, their pardons and dispensations with which they sweep up everything. Three things never satiate the Romans: the *pallium*, the pontifical months, and the annats.

' " Each year they strive to extort more. Thus the *pallium* of the Archbishop of Mayence formerly cost 10,000 florins, now it costs 20,000; and in the space of a man's life, we have seen it eight times renewed. The six months which have been given to the Pope, in the event of the vacancy of a benefice, are also in the same way raised to a year. And not even this suffices them. They sell benefices publicly, and have no scruple in selling them to two or three competitors at the same time. What does it matter to them, whether or not they have the canonical qualifications? Dispensations, suffice for everything : they make of a child, and a woman, a man who has attained the years of majority. The Romans sin without dispensation; but they sell to others the pardon of their sins.

' " If one wishes to obtain anything at Rome, he must provide himself with three things : money, introductions, falsehood. Three things will supply the place of money : personal beauty, corruption of heart, and patience in addition to both. Three things may reclaim Rome to virtue : the energetic resolution of the princes, the impatience of the nations, and the victories of the Turks. Nevertheless, it is not necessary to cut off the head of the church : it suffices to extirpate her corruptions; a painful operation, doubtless, and one which cannot be effected without violence. When the head shall be cured, the body will do well. The priests, less numerous, less rich, and better employed, will lead more holy lives; they will marry respectable women, instead of maintaining shameless concubines. This indispensable reform has always failed owing to the fault of sovereigns, and the ignorance of nations. It is therefore time that these abuses should come to an end. Let us no longer endure that Rome shall oppress us by a false appearance of holiness; that she shall impose upon us, as the infallible laws of the church, the bulls which the Pope fabricates with some favourite associates; and that she shall despoil us by means of her indulgences, or under the most lying pretexts. The successors of St Peter ought, indeed, to fish, but souls, and not treasures; for no communion can exist between Christ and Belial. Christ has said, Blessed are the poor; for theirs is the kingdom of heaven! But as for them, they say: To the rich is the kingdom of heaven; for the Pope and his agents go everywhere preaching and proclaiming that we participate in the kingdom of heaven, just in proportion to the number of indulgences which we buy. And as to all the dispensations sold by the legates! They release from the most sacred oaths, from the holiest duties, from the penalties which have been deserved by the most execrable crimes.

' " Three things are incessantly going on at Rome, and never finished: the canonization of saints, the building of churches, and the war against the Turks. Of three things it is forbidden to speak ill: the Pope, indulgences, and impiety. Three classes of people bear rule at Rome: ruffians, courtesans, and usurers. Three things are pompously apparelled: prelates, mules, and women of the town. Of three things they boast at Rome, although they possess them not: piety, faith, and innocence. And three things exist, of which they boast not: traffic in offices, the venality of justice, and treachery in friendship. To his two swords, the Pope adds a third, with which he shears his flock and flays them till the blood flows.

' " Such is the impure source from which a flood of corruption and misery has flowed down upon every nation; and will not all the nations understand that it must be stopped up? Will they not come by land and sea with fire and sword? Oh, Rome! all Christendom has her eyes fixed upon thee; what thou dost appears to all honourable and lawful. It is on this account that thy corruption has tainted everything. Thou hast gathered together, as in a reservoir, the spoils of an entire universe; and thou hast given them to be consumed by a crowd of parasites. First they have drained our blood, then they have eaten our flesh; now they have come to the very marrow of our bones, and still they are not satiated! And yet the Germans would hesitate to have recourse to arms! These are the spoilers of our country: we defray the expense of all their vices. With the money of which they plunder us, they maintain their dogs, their horses, their mistresses. We pay for the purple that clothes them, for the marble palaces in which they dwell. And now they threaten, they insult us; they forbid us to hesitate, to murmur at their intolerable exactions. They wish, along with our money, our shame and our smiles. When shall we have eyes to see our humiliation and our ruin, and arms to avenge them?"' [1]

———◆———

XVII.

THE *Trias Romana* produced an immense sensation in Germany. 'By this pamphlet,' says Cochlæus, Hutten has made the name of the Roman court the most detested in Germany.' And it is principally to it that we must attribute the expression of popular opinion which, as we have already seen, burst forth against the legates in 1519 and 1520.

The fame of it reached even to Rome, and procured for Hutten, for the first time, the honour of the pontifical wrath. But before the Pope had fulminated an anathema against him, Hutten had already acquired a fresh title to his implacable hatred. He printed, in June 1520, several letters, written at the end of the fourteenth century by the most illustrious Universities, upon the means of putting an end to the schism in the church. His preface terminates by the noble

[1] I have given a summary of this pamphlet, principally following Meiners. I cannot cite all which I borrow from that excellent book.

motto which he adopted after the publication of the
Trias Romana, 'Long live liberty! The die is cast!'
His principal aim in publishing these letters, was
to point out with what freedom the ancient Universities had discussed the rights of nations, of the
Emperor, of councils, and the illegal power of the
Popes.   He wished to arouse, by that example, the
emulation of the principal schools of his time, and
to protest against the condemnation pronounced by
the Universities of Cologne and of Louvain against
Luther.   He cites, at the end of his preface, that
beautiful saying of St Gregory : ' We must remind
subjects, that they must not be too submissive ;
otherwise they would come to venerate even the
vices of their masters.'   And to the court of Rome
he made the application of that great and everlast-
ing reservation in favour of justice !

This work was published in the castle of
Steckelberg.   The boldness of the *Trias Romana*,
printed at Mayence, had undoubtedly overpassed
the limits which the Archbishop wished to put to
his adhesion to the new ideas.   Shortly afterwards,
the Archbishop received a brief from the Pope, who,
with all the deference due to such an important
personage, expressed his astonishment and grief at
learning that there had been printed in his arch-
bishopric, and almost under his eyes, such enor-
mities, and exhorted him to punish the insolence

of a *certain* Hutten,[1] that his chastisement may
serve as a warning and example to others. Albert
did not follow the injunction of the Pope to the
letter, but he demanded of Hutten a promise to
write nothing more against the court of Rome.
Hutten refused to enslave his conscience, and the
Archbishop, under pain of excommunication, pro-
hibited the reading of the writings of Hutten, and
other such fellows. 'This,' writes Luther, 'is undoubtedly directed against me. If he had named
me, I would have answered in such a way as to
cure him of the wish of attacking me. By these
violences, they themselves prepare the way for the
end of their tyranny.'

Hutten having no longer any hope of assistance
from the Archbishop of Mayence, and freed from
the restraints which that hope imposed upon him,
hastened to ally himself with Luther. He had
already appreciated the importance of the mission
which that great man was called upon to fulfil.
He had comprehended that the monkish quarrel,
at which he had formerly laughed, contained the
germ of that very revolution to which all his own
energies were directed. He had, in common with
all Germany, been charmed, carried away, and sub-

---

[1] This presumption of style was usual with the Roman court. In
the bull against Luther, we read in the same way, ' *a certain* Luther.'
Hutten puts, as a note upon this word, *Attende emphasin.*

dued by the burning words of the Doctor of Wittemberg, and with the glance of an experienced man,
with the modesty of a hero, he had hailed in
Luther the chief of the Reformation. After 1519,
he had caused to be made to him the offer of a
secure asylum with Sickingen. In June 1520, he
himself thus wrote to him :—

' Long live liberty ! Ulrich von Hutten, knight,
to Martin Luther, theologian. If you meet with
some difficulties in the great enterprises which you
undertake with such unshaken courage, be assured
that I am with you, heart and soul. And, for myself, I do not remain idle. May Christ be with us
and assist us, since we restore, you with more success, I according to my abilities, His divine laws ;
and may He bring us back to the light of His
doctrine, falsified and veiled in darkness by the
pontifical constitutions. Would to God that all
would feel like us, and that our adversaries
would themselves recognise their injustice, and
return to the right way ! They say that you are
excommunicated. How much, O Luther, would
that ennoble you ! All truly religious men would
say with you, " They have enchained the word of
the Just One, and have condemned innocent blood ;
but the Lord our God will punish them for their
injustice, and will cause them to perish in their
iniquity." There is our hope and our faith. Eck

returns from Rome, overwhelmed, it is said, with money and benefices; and afterwards? The sinner is praised in his plans; but may the Lord direct us in His truth! .... However, be upon your guard, and withdraw not your attention or your mind from the designs of your persecutors. If you should now perish, you must yourself feel what a public calamity that would be! I well know that your courage is such, that you would prefer to die thus, rather than continue to live as you have hitherto done. Me they equally threaten, and I have determined to take all possible precautions: if they employ force, I shall oppose it with force, equal, I trust, if not superior; yet I sincerely desire that they may deem me beneath their notice. Eck has denounced me as belonging to your party: and in that he has spoken the truth; for I have always gone along with you in all that I have known of you. But, up to the present time, we have never had any connection: he has then lied when he has said, in order to please the Pope, that we act in conformity to a plan previously agreed upon between us. What a wicked and insolent man! As to yourself, remain firm, and hesitate not in the path on which you have entered. In every engagement I shall be your second: you may then confide to me all your ulterior projects. Let us unite to save liberty; let us set free our country, so

long oppressed.   The Lord is with us; who, then,
shall be against us? . . . . I set out to-day to
present myself to Ferdinand. I shall spare nothing,
and shall make the greatest exertions to forward
the interests of our cause. Sickingen invites you to
come to him, if you are not in safety where you are
at present: he will welcome you as you deserve,
and will protect you against every enemy.   He has
several times requested me to write to you.'

This letter appears to have been printed immediately, with the exception of the name of Sickingen, which is left blank in the edition which is
before me: they wished, doubtless, not to divulge
beforehand the asylum offered to Luther.   It appears to have made a great impression upon the
illustrious Reformer.   Henceforth he found himself
more free, and less obliged to moderate the impetuosity of his generous anger, as he had hitherto
done, out of regard to the Elector of Saxony.   It is
at this time (December 1520) that he published
his *Captivity of Babylon*, and his *Appeal to the Christian Nobility of the German Nation for the Reformation of the Church*.

XVIII.

UTTEN set out, full of hope, for Brabant, where Ferdinand held his court while waiting for the arrival of his brother, Charles V. The young Emperor was about to visit the Empire. It appeared impossible that Charles V., elected in spite of the Pope, and who seemed to wear so loftily all the crowns united on his head, should not seize the opportunity, unique in history, of terminating to his own advantage the war between the secular empire and the priesthood, and of reforming the abuses under which the church was sinking. The favour which Sickingen enjoyed at his court increased still further these hopes; for no one was ignorant of the ties which linked that noble knight—in whom Germany honoured another Bayard—to the friends of the new learning. But where Hutten saw encouragement given to a fervent partisan of reform, there was only a political calculation. Charles V. wished to attach to himself a man who was the most brilliant representative of ancient chivalry, iron arm and lion heart, whom the whole German nobility hailed as its hero and its model. To do so was to gain, in the very heart of Germany, an important basis of defence against the princes, who, for a century, had directed all their efforts to form in the

Empire a kind of constitutional oligarchy. As to
the Pope, if Charles V. had only been Emperor, he
would undoubtedly have boldly treated him as his
enemy; for, in spite of his Spanish education, we
cannot suppose the man who afterwards let loose
against Rome the Lutheran bands of Freundsberg
(29) to have been troubled with many religious
scruples. But at this moment, as the Pope might
be useful to his designs upon Italy, he sacrificed
to him Germany. Hutten rapidly comprehended
the motives of a policy which was to result in the
Edict of Worms; but, faithful to the ideal which he
had formed of the Emperor, he preferred to impute
to his youth and inexperience, abused by detestable
advisers, a conduct dictated by a genius which was
profoundly calculating in the very age of passion.

Hutten could not remain long at court. On his
arrival, he was warned that the legates had designs
upon his life, and that they had hired assassins to
make away with him, by dagger or by poison. His
friends entreated him to be gone. He resisted for
a long time; but he was at length obliged to yield
to the evidence of facts, and to depart in all haste.
At Mayence, they believed him dead, and his return
was celebrated as a resurrection. He learned at
Frankfort, that the Pope had written to several of
the princes, to request them to seize and send him
prisoner to Rome: that demand had been especially

directed to the Archbishop of Mayence. Finally, the legate asked the Emperor to put Hutten to the ban of the Empire, and to permit the agents of the Roman court to seize his person, wherever they might find him.

These circumstances created a kind of solitude around Hutten. The feeblest among his friends denied him : the others withdrew. As to himself, in this moment of extreme danger, he became but the more determined to defend the truth, to vindicate the liberty of his country—' for which,' he says, ' it is my duty to die.' His friend Sickingen gave him, in his castle of Ebernburg, a retreat inaccessible to all violence, to all treason. From thence, as from another Wartburg, this worthy brother in arms of Luther continued to issue his fiery publications.

This time, he relied upon the injury done to himself, and made it the text of an energetic appeal to the liberty and the honour of Germany. As in the outset of his career, he raised his private affairs to the elevation of a great national cause, and excited all minds by the vehemence of his protestations.

He writes to his former protector, the Archbishop of Mayence : [1] ' I have learned through others what

---

[1] This letter, and those which follow, are brought together in a collection which bears on the title-page the motto, *Jacta est alea*, and which finishes by that verse of the psalmist—*Dirumpamus vincula eorum et projiciamus a nobis jugum ipsorum.*

Leo X. has demanded of you,—by what commands, what force, he presses you to send me in fetters to Rome. I ought, perhaps, to have waited until warned by yourself. Without doubt, you fear the Pope. I hope that you are the better for such condescension; but I am very much afraid that, by pretensions hitherto unheard of, he prepares for all of you, bishops and priests, some disastrous, some atrocious blow. Think of this, and take your precautions in time. More than ever it is necessary that I should be able to maintain my communications with you; and nothing is more painful to me, in my present position, than not being able to do so. I am shut out from courts, from towns, from all public life, from all human society; and for what crime? Because I have defended the truth, and advised what is good. They have condemned me unheard, and they only wish to have me at Rome in order to put me to death. Who, then, with a drop of German blood in his veins, would not have risen against such indignities? Yes, I despise, I detest all these inventions of the Bishops of Rome. They are not inspired by God, but by the love of gain. I brave their anger, their excommunications, and their poisons; my help is in the Lord, the Creator of heaven and earth.' (September 1520.)

To his old friend, the knight von Rotenhan, he writes: ' What think you of this thunderbolt launched against me? What are your hopes, your expectations of the future? When they attack me, dare you defend me? Have you still the heart of a Franconian, a love for the ancient liberty of our country? No, Germany is not so abandoned of Heaven, that many will not join with me to carry out that great enterprise, which cannot longer be deferred without ruin to our liberty, without ruin to every true Christian. If I remain alone, I shall find a refuge in my own conscience, and shall console myself by the hope of a near futurity; for the flame which I have kindled, cannot be so thoroughly extinguished as to prevent its bursting forth anew, more terrible than ever. Watch, therefore, the course of events with care: sound the intentions of the nobility. As to my foes, tell them that I am disheartened: they will perhaps despise me. I make my complaint to the Emperor, to the princes, to the nations of Germany, not that I fear for myself, but that I wish to raise public opinion in favour of the cause of liberty, by exposing the unheard-of iniquity of the conduct of the Romanists. The Pope invokes against me the aid of the secular arm, and, for my part, I invoke the goodness of the Lord! How will all this end? You may form conjectures; but this is certain, that we shall attempt something, and that we shall not manage the affair like cowards.' (September 1520.)

Of the same date, he addressed a letter to Charles V., in which he insists upon the insult offered to the imperial dignity by the claim put forward by the Pope, to order a German knight, a member of the body of which the Emperor is the head, to be brought in chains to Rome, without trial or judgment. 'And for what crime? They themselves confess that there is none. But for what reason? Because I have proclaimed the Christian truth, protested against the novel inventions of the Pope, vindicated the ancient liberty of the Empire, and especially because I have diminished their receipts, and the profits of their spoliation. If this is a crime, let me, at least, be judged and punished by you, my only sovereign. What would become of Germany, if we could no longer, either serve you without peril, or undertake without danger the affairs of the country? And what would become of religion, if we were forced to put the paltry Romanist traditions above the divine commands? Would to God you could behold what indignation that violence excites, with what passion we await, at your hands, justice and vengeance! Each one feels himself threatened. Is it not truly an atrocious, an unheard-of thing, to wish to chain a man, to torture him, to kill without hearing him? (30.) Yes, I have attacked, I shall unceasingly attack, the enemies of the truth, the oppressors of public liberty, the maligners of your dignity. It is my duty to watch over your dignity; my religion, to love my country. In all this, I have no private interest to serve. Truly, my conscience vindicates me, and I have confidence in your justice. Your interest is mine, my cause yours; if you abandon me, you are lost. After that first concession, you can no longer refuse anything to their insatiable pretensions; else they will overthrow you, as they have overthrown so many of your predecessors. What have they not wrested from the Empire by stratagem and by force? They have made emperors kiss their feet; they have imposed upon them the oath of vassalage. They ruin your Empire by their exactions. They sell indulgences, absolutions, dispensations,—a traffic infamous from its objects, more infamous still by the artifices of those who carry it on. They anathematize the best of your subjects; some of them they have poisoned, others they have delivered over to their enemies. They fan the flame of discord among the German princes. Such has been their work hitherto. One thing only remains: to compel the delivery to them of those Germans who have incurred their displeasure. Such is what they now demand. Think of your dignity, of the majesty of the Empire, of my own rank! Judge my cause yourself. What can a German knight have to do with the Bishop of Rome?'

Sickingen transmitted this letter to Charles V., who promised that Hutten should not be delivered up, without being brought to trial.

XIX.

ANOTHER letter, addressed to the princes, the nobles, and the people of Germany, reproduced the same considerations, the same eloquent complaints. But the most important document of this collection, is that addressed to Frederick of Saxony, the moderate but resolute protector of Luther. It is quite a manifesto.

'The moment is come, Prince Frederick, to oppose the tyranny of Rome. In spite of so many brotherly warnings, the Romanists, instead of exhibiting more moderation, have only become still more violent. You know that they wish that I should be sent to Rome in fetters. And as to Luther? What a cruel and violent bull have they launched against him! The roaring of the lion, who has made all the flock of Christ to tremble! Where can we trace the least mildness or apostolical moderation? More atrocious still, when the Pope enwraps himself, in that bull, in the mantle of Christian benevolence, and, in dulcet tones, invites

Luther to come to Rome. Luther at Rome! But do we not know, only too well, what they would do to us, if Luther should go there voluntarily, and I should be brought there by force? As to myself, I wonder how Leo has been able to persuade himself that it would be so easy to rid himself of me, and to drag me to Rome! And then, what conduct for a pastor, for a bishop, for a vicar of Christ, to condemn a Christian to capital punishment without judging him, without even hearing him! And what crime of ours excites his fury against us? We have striven to bring to light the Christian doctrine, obscured and almost effaced by his rapacity. Our nation is the best fitted for liberty, and we cannot resign ourselves to behold her enslaved. This is what displeases that good shepherd; but this also is pleasing to Christ. We cannot, at the same time, serve Christ and the Pope, our country and her oppressors. Peace cannot subsist between him and us; for peace is between us and truth!

'The moment has arrived when the strife can be no longer deferred. Their perversity and our misery are at their height. The day approaches when that great Babylon, the mother of corruptions and abominations, shall fall;—I would say, that See of Rome, sullied by every crime, and which, hostile to all the institutions of Christ, pretends to hold the place of Christ, which, full of lust, and glutted with the blood of the earth, does not the less hold up to the eyes of the faithful the keys which open and shut heaven, with a confidence so complete, that she fears not to sell us consecrated things, or to forbid us their use, according to her caprice. I seem to hear a heavenly voice, which commands us to attack, to destroy that hundred-headed beast : Shall her crimes still go on increasing? And if they are at their height, ought they not at length to be punished?

' But who shall overthrow that detestable structure? Who shall reform these vices? Who wash away these pollutions? God? Yes, doubtless, but by the instrumentality of man. What are you then about, O Princes? What advice, what assistance do you offer us? You especially, to whom belongs the hereditary right to defend the liberties of Germany : you, the chief of these noble Saxons whom no foreigner has ever subdued ! the chief of the country of Arminius, of the Henry's and of the Otho's ! Would to God that you, who have the power, possessed also our boldness ; or that we, who have the boldness, possessed your power ! As to me, I shall not cease to exhort you, until you have recovered your ancient virtue, or until I see that you are no longer capable of doing so. Then I shall betake myself elsewhere. If the head of the nation fails to support this great cause, the arms shall not also be wanting !'

'But cannot we emancipate ourselves without
bloodshed? May that blood be on the heads of
those who will not give up their injustice and
tyranny! Let us strike with the sword, if so it
must be, those who have so often made use of the
sword. Perhaps it will not be necessary to go this
length. There is a certain means to destroy the
Roman tyranny: let us keep our money. Afterwards, under another Otho, we shall purge the city
of Rome and its senate; we shall restore to the
Emperor the capital of the Empire; we shall bring
down the Pope to the level of the other bishops;
we shall diminish the number and the revenues of
the priests, we shall scarcely retain one out of a
hundred. As to those who call themselves *friars*,
and who live only by disputes, we shall entirely
suppress them. Then no one shall enter into the
ranks of the clergy through effeminacy or love of
money; and all those hypocritical monks shall
cease to deceive the people, and to beg the sweat
and the blood of the poor!'

'In destroying the convents, in cutting off all
the avenues by which our money finds its way to
Rome, we shall acquire a variety of resources for
useful employment: we shall then be able to raise
armies against the Turks, to maintain the many
unfortunates whom hunger drives to theft, to protect the sciences, to assist the miserable, to en-

courage virtue.   Then we shall give one hand to
the Bohemians, who have freed themselves before
us from that rapacious spawn, and the other to the
Greeks, who have separated themselves from the
Roman tyranny.'

‘ They will say that this is to overwhelm the
bark of St Peter, to rend the coat without seam :
such is the habitual theme of their declamations.
But you must clearly perceive that, far from sup-
pressing charity, I earnestly wish to enlarge its
sphere, by chasing away those who are obstacles to
its operation.   Far from destroying the church, I
open its arms to all Christians : instead of these corrupted Romanists, these buttresses of Antichrist, I
would entrust the priesthood to those recommended
by the purity of their lives.   The drones removed,
the bees will come of themselves.'

‘ For my part, if I do not succeed in gaining
you over to this noble enterprise, nor in elsewhere kindling the fire which shall purify that
corruption, I shall at least do nothing unworthy
of a knight.   Never shall I retreat a hair's breadth
from anything that I have spoken ; I shall remain
free, for I fear not death.   Hutten will never become the slave of a foreign sovereign, however
great he may be, and of the Pope less than any
other ; for I would consider it dishonouring to
me, and a calling down of the divine wrath,

if I adored along with you the hundred-headed beast!'

'And now, I quit towns, because I cannot forsake the truth; I live in solitude, because I cannot live free in society. For the rest, I am full of contempt for the dangers which threaten me; for I can die, but not be a slave. I cannot endure with patience the yoke borne by my country. But one day, perhaps, I shall emerge from my retreat; I shall arrive in the midst of the assembled multitude, and I shall cry out to my fellow-citizens, "Who will live and die with Hutten for liberty?"' (September 1520).

Luther, in sending this letter to Spalatin, to be transmitted to the Elector, adds, 'Good God! what will be the end of all these novelties! I begin to believe that the Papacy, hitherto invincible, will be overthrown, contrary to all expectation, or else the last day approaches.'

XX.

HUTTEN had long believed that the union of the Emperor, of the nobles, of the learned men and intelligent burgesses of the great towns, might, without any revolu-

tionary movement, effect a pacific reformation of
the church, and bring about the foundation of a
national church upon the ruins of that of Rome;
for it is to these two objects that his thoughts seem
at first to have been limited, and his polemical
writings directed. He therefore wrote in the Latin
language, 'in order to give,' as he himself says,
'my counsels in some degree in secret. I have
not been anxious to address myself to the people,
although I had so many inducements to do so.'
But he soon saw that nothing could be effected
without a great movement of public opinion. He
could no longer delude himself either with re-
liance on the Archbishop of Mayence, who had
abandoned his cause, or on Charles V., who had
allied himself to the Pope, or on the princes, who
all followed their private ends. He comprehended
that he must seek elsewhere the support which the
great and powerful refused him.

In September 1520, he published a translation
of his letter to the Elector of Saxony; and a little
later, he sent forth among the people a poem in
German, under the title, '*Complaint and Warning
against the excessive, antichristian Power of the Pope,
and against the Godlessness of the Monastic Orders.
Written in verse by Ulrich von Hutten, Poet and
Orator, for the good of all Christendom, and especially
of Germany, his native country. The die is cast. I*

have dared it.' Let us conceive the impassioned
and too true accusations of the *Trias Romana*,—
its invocations to patriotism, to glory, to oppressed
liberty,—its ardent protestations against Romish
tyranny and corruption, thrown among a people
who had just begun to read some of the writings of
Luther, and who had hitherto possessed scarcely
any other intellectual nourishment than the ro-
mances of chivalry; and we shall comprehend the
effect produced by Hutten's poem. Certainly, we
need not search there for the poetic ideal; but the
rhyme, united to the popular clearness of thought,
doubled its effect and fixed it in the memory.
Thus, the poorest bought the poem, the most
ignorant understood it; everywhere, even in the
most remote hamlets, some one was found to repeat to the deeply-moved commonalty the words
of freedom. This immense and truly popular success, attested by an infinite number of editions
which succeeded each other from month to month,
and some of which continued to appear even to the
middle of the seventeenth century, was, indeed, all
that Hutten had hoped for. 'Up to this time,' he
says, 'I had written in Latin; I was not understood
by every one. Now I invoke the fatherland in the
national language. You must blow away from before your eyes the smoke which blinds you. If
you would follow my advice, fellow-countrymen,

you would very speedily purge the Gospel of all these Romish fables.'

After what I have said of the preceding writings of Hutten, and especially of the *Trias Romana*, I need not delay long upon this German poem. What is new in it, is not the thought, but the form, the language, the rhyme, the appeal to the people. However, I must mention two things, which will give us an accurate conception of the nature of the ideas which at this moment occupied the mind of Hutten. The first is the justification of John Huss, which will be soon followed by that of Ziska.

'They have burned Huss,' he says, 'because he held to the teaching of Christ without attending to the glosses of the priests; because he denounced their avarice, their pride, their luxury, the tyranny of the Pope, and all his thefts from Christians, and the constitution of the canon law, opposed in every point to the Scriptures. These denunciations were true then, and are true now. The priests, however, were stirred up to vengeance. Huss was cited before them, with a safe-conduct from the Emperor; but Sigismund kept his word as so many princes still do. He suffered himself to be led away by the advice of the priests, which also condemned Christ. They told him that he was not bound to keep faith with a heretic. But, although it might be true that Huss was a heretic, a crime

was not the less committed, in condemning him
in spite of his safe-conduct. Nor was Jerome of
Prague any more spared. Since that time, none
have followed their example: all have feared the
stake.'

I shall next cite the conclusion of the poem,
which contains a direct call to arms :—'How can
we endure such a tyranny? I affirm that we
ought not to do so. The time is come. God
has reserved for our age the liberation of our
fatherland. I hope that King Charles will be on
our side, that he will not give himself up to oppression. I summon to that work the princes, the
nobles, and all those who wish to crush the heresy
of the Pope. He who would remain indifferent to
this great enterprise, loves not his country, and
knows not the true God! We wish to abolish
superstition, to restore truth. And since that cannot be done peacefully, it may well be necessary
that blood shall flow. As to myself, I have recoiled
before that extremity, I have believed that we
might attain our object by another path. But
we must do what we can. The hour has sounded:
we have already submitted to too many insults.
Rally round me, Germans; be of good cheer. We
have plenty of hauberks and horses, of halberts and
swords; and, since pacific counsels are useless, let
us fly to arms! The help and the vengeance of

God are on our side! Our enemies are the enemies
of God! Let my words awaken the princes in their
courts, the knights in their castles, the burgesses in
their towns! Who would stay inactive at home,
in so good a cause! For my own part, I have
dared the peril, that is my device!'

In the same year, 1520—that year so fruitful in
Hutten's life, so important in the history of the Reformation, in which Luther published his book on
the Captivity of Babylon, and burned the Pope's
bull and the decretals in the public square at Wittemberg—Hutten translated into German several of
his dialogues, and especially the *Trias Romana*, and
published them, with a dedication to *The noble,
famous, courageous, and very honourable Councillor,
servant and captain of His Majesty the Emperor,
Francis of Sickingen, my well beloved friend and con-
soler.* I may perhaps be mistaken; but I think that
we find in these pages something of the touching
accents of Montaigne, when speaking of La Boëtie.

' It is not without reason that the proverb says:
In adversity we come to know our friends! for no
one can be assured of having a friend, if he has
not proved him during adversity, so as thoroughly
to know him. Although those are to be esteemed
happy who have not required thus to test their
friends, those also may thank God who have found,
in their misfortunes, a faithful and steady friend.

More than any one, therefore, I ought to bless God and my destiny. For, attacked by my enemies in my property, my person, and my honour, with such violence, that I have scarcely had time to summon my friends to my assistance, you have come to my aid, not, as often happens, with words of consolation only, but also with effective help. . .

. . . It is not that I despise those who are our friends in the time of prosperity (although that may be termed an agreeable acquaintanceship rather than a true friendship); but I make between the two the same distinction that physicians make amongst meats: some are merely savoury; others are also salutary. And thus, Heaven has bestowed you upon me, when I had need both of help and of cure. From the love of truth, and from compassion for my misfortunes, you have espoused my cause without caring about my enemies. And when, through the imminence of the danger, the cities were closed against me, you have opened to me your castles, which I shall call on this, and on other accounts, *the abodes of justice.*'

' Besides, I found myself not a little strengthened in my purpose, when I saw that you also regarded it as just and honourable. And all the learned men of Germany, who are menaced in my person, have taken courage; whilst the Romanists, who, believing me entirely overthrown, already celebrated their triumph, have become discouraged, on finding me supported by an impregnable wall. In order to prove to you my gratitude, it is not heart that I want, or will, but happiness and ability; but, at least, I give you that of which none can deprive me, the strength of my soul and of my intellect.

'I offer you, then, for your New Year's gift, my little books, which I have translated into German, in this abode of justice.   And I wish for you, not, as is often wished, a life of tranquillity and repose, but just, serious, noble, and laborious affairs, in which, for the good of mankind, you may have an opportunity of displaying your heroic heart. May God give you happiness and safety.

'Written at Ebernburg on New Year's evening' (31st December 1520).

XXI.

THE relations between Hutten and Luther became more and more intimate: they communicated to each other their plans, their fears, and their hopes, and drew from these frequent communications, new strength and firmer courage.   In the opening of the year 1521, Hutten wrote that beautiful letter *to his dearest brother and friend, Martin Luther, the invincible herald of the word of God.* 'You would,' he says, 'assuredly compassionate me, if you knew all the opposition against which I have to contend. Whilst I seek to attach new friends to our cause,[1] many of the old ones fall away from it: so much are the souls of men still under the dominion of that prejudice, that to attack the Pope is to commit an unpardonable crime. Francis of Sickingen alone remains faithful to us; and they have almost succeeded in shaking even his fidelity, by showing him, as coming from you, monstrous things, which you certainly have never written. I have effaced that impression by reading your works to him, with which, until the present moment, he was very little acquainted. He has not been slow to appreciate them, and, beholding the grandeur of your undertaking, he has exclaimed, filled with admiration, "Is it really possible that a single man has the courage to attack all the past; and if he has sufficient courage, will he have sufficient power?" He is so full of enthusiasm for the

---

[1] It is important to observe, that Hutten did not admit all the doctrines of Luther. The theory of predestination instinctively repelled him; but he knew that if the Romanists opposed Luther, it was less on account of his dogmatic opinions than on account of his violent invectives against their corruption and rapacity. 'Thus,' as he himself says, 'I accept the title of Lutheran, in order that they may know that I am ever faithful to the cause of truth and liberty.'

cause, that scarcely an evening passes without his requesting me to read to him one or other of our books.   His friends advise him to abandon so perilous a path.   "No," he exclaims, "the cause which I defend is neither dangerous nor doubtful.   It is the cause of God and of truth: it is the fatherland itself which commands us to listen to the counsels of Luther and of Hutten, and to maintain the true faith."   However, I ought not to conceal from you, that Sickingen has hitherto prevented me from taking any active steps against our enemies.   He believes that we must wait the judgment of the Emperor, and what may be decided with regard to our affairs after the Diet of Worms.   So far as I am concerned, I have little confidence in the Emperor: he is always surrounded by priests, and selects from among them his most cherished councillors.   They take advantage of his youth, and urge him to adopt measures which, certainly, will not be for his advantage.   Sickingen, on the contrary, believes that the Emperor will decide, as he ought to do, at Worms, with regard to these faithless Popes and their supporters.   Many even predict, that at that Diet, a complete rupture will take place between the Pope and the Emperor; and you may rely upon it that Sickingen will lend all his influence to bring this about, and he has great credit with the Emperor. . . . . They have thrice burnt your books!

But what matters it?   The people gather more
courage every day.   Throughout the whole country
your name is never pronounced without veneration,
whilst Aleander (31) was nearly being stoned at
Mayence.   I have written to Spalatin, to induce
him to endeavour to ascertain the designs of your
prince : endeavour yourself, I entreat you, to ascertain these.   It would be a great point for us to
learn that, in case of need, he would come to our
assistance, or at least would give us an asylum in
his states.   As soon as I shall be assured on this
point, I shall fly to you ; because I cannot resist my
desire to see at length a man whom I love so much
for his virtues.'

———————◆———————

XXII.

THE Diet of Worms had a decisive influence
upon subsequent events.   It drove, it
compelled to violence, a revolution which
had hitherto been purely pacific, and which bade fair
to transform the whole face of Germany by the
force of argument alone.   We do not, then, depart
from our subject when we pause for a little to consider it.   Besides, we shall thus contemplate one
of the most magnificent scenes in the drama of history.

We have seen that, for Charles V., the question which agitated Germany, which shook to its deepest foundations the ancient fabric of Christian Europe, resolved itself into a somewhat paltry calculation of a purely material policy. Luther might serve him, either to hold the Pope in check, or to reward him for his alliance. This policy was frankly avowed by the imperial minister to the nuncio who brought him the bulls against Luther: 'The Emperor will exert himself to the uttermost to do what is agreeable to the Pope, if on his side the Pope will show himself the friend of the Emperor, and will not negotiate with his enemies.' At Rome this was perfectly well understood. They therefore never attempted to work upon the conscience of Charles V.: they appealed to his interests alone; and employed means even still less justifiable. They put at the disposition of the legate Aleander, all the means of corruption which appeared to him likely to be successful in gaining over the ministers of the Emperor and in bribing the Diet. He bestowed on a bishop, who had great influence at court, a benefice already promised to another; he paid a secretary of the Emperor for *good* and *secret services ;* he even went the length of bribing the door-keepers, in order that they might intercept Luther's books. And he made a parade of all these villanies with the most barefaced impudence. He boasted of having obtained, by cunning and activity, that the works of Luther should be burned in Flanders. ' The Emperor and his councillors,' he exclaimed, ' will see the glare of the pile before they clearly understand that they have given the order to kindle it.'

The ability of this man was not, as we shall see, without its effect in obtaining the famous Edict of Worms. As to Charles V., they made sure of his concurrence in the following manner :—The Cortes of Arragon, after long efforts, had succeeded in obtaining a papal brief which modified the organization and the procedure of the Inquisition, and assimilated them to the common law. The Inquisition was the chief pillar of the Spanish crown ; all that tended to diminish its implacable and arbitrary rigour appeared to Charles V. to threaten the stability of his throne. He therefore vehemently protested against the papal brief. The Pope revoked it ; and, in return, the Emperor engaged to execute the bull against Luther (32). An instructive and curious reconciliation : religious despotism clasps the hand of political tyranny ; the suspension of all progress in Spain, is the price of the suppression of the Reformation movement in Germany. There is an intimate connection between all liberties, and between all despotisms !

But in Germany, nothing could be done without

the Diet. They feared its opposition; because, for a century past, it had never assembled without directing against the corruptions of the Church, remonstrances which were always useless, but whose energy was constantly increasing. They wished to make short work of the matter. Accordingly, one day, when a tournament had been announced, and all the preparations made, the Emperor suddenly summoned the princes together, and read to them the bull against Luther, and the edict which was to put it into execution. We may imagine the excitement which this unexpected proceeding produced among the assemblage. The Emperor wished immediately to publish the edict, according to the advice of the theologians, Aleander and Eck. 'He is condemned,' said they; 'what further is required?' But the Diet was more difficult to satisfy. Although, perhaps, the majority were not opposed to the condemnation, they felt strongly that that condemnation, pronounced in the absence of Luther, and without his having had an opportunity of defending himself, would be an outrage to the public conscience. They demanded that Luther should be cited, that he should have a safe-conduct, that he should be heard; declaring, besides, that they would accept the edict if Luther persisted, not in his attacks against the corruptions of the church (on that point all were agreed with him), but 'in his doctrines, contrary to the faith which our fathers and ancestors have transmitted to us.'

The citation was given with this understanding, and an imperial herald repaired to Wittemberg to seek Luther. Many hoped that that great man would retract, that he would content himself with insisting on the reformation of the church, so popular in Germany, and in fact so generally desired. But Luther had other designs: no consideration, no seduction, no personal fear, could make him desert what he considered to be the truth.

He set out immediately in a carriage, with which the town of Wittemberg furnished him. By the way, he could read on all the walls the imperial mandate which condemned his books. This was well calculated to inspire apprehension; and the imperial herald himself, distrusting the safe-conduct, asked him at Weimar, whether he would not desire to return. At the first halting-place, a councillor of his patron, the Elector of Saxony, came to him to say, that it would be better for him not to go farther, as he ran the risk of experiencing the fate of Huss. To all which the Reformer replied, 'Huss has perished, but not the truth. I shall go, if I should have against me as many devils as there are tiles on the house-tops of Worms!'

On Thursday, the 16th April 1521, at mid-day, the warden of the gate-tower sounded the trumpet, to announce the arrival of Luther. The crowd threw itself upon his path. He sat in his carriage bareheaded, and in his monkish dress; before him rode the imperial herald with his tabard, embroidered with the imperial eagle, hanging over his arm. Luther contemplated the excited, agitated crowd with a serene countenance. He read in all eyes sympathy for his cause; his courage rose to confidence; and when he descended from his carriage, he cried, 'God will be with me.'

On the morrow, he was summoned before the Diet. The assembly was numerous and splendid. The Emperor, surrounded by six electors, by all the lay and ecclesiastical princes, by the deputies from the cities, and by the most illustrious captains and councillors, expected Luther with visible curiosity. At the sight of so magnificent an assemblage, the poor monk could not master his emotion. He spoke in a low, suffocated, almost unintelligible voice: many believed that he was terrified. He was asked if he was willing to defend all that was to be found in his books, or to retract something. He demanded delay for reflection. He was granted twenty-four hours.

Next day he again appeared. It was late; night had fallen; the torches were lighted. The assembly was still more numerous than on the previous occasion; and the concourse of people was so great, that the princes scarcely found room to seat themselves. But now Luther was master of himself: his conscience gave him courage to raise his head in the presence of those princes before whom all bent the knee; he, too, felt himself a power, and desired to honour by his attitude the truth, of which he was the organ. There was no longer any trembling in his voice, any hesitation in his answers. When they repeated the question of the previous day, he replied in a firm, manly voice, everywhere audible. He divided his books into books of doctrine, books against the abuses of the See of Rome, and polemical books. 'To retract the first is impossible, since the bull itself finds much that is good in them; to retract the second, would be to furnish the Romanists with the means of completely crushing Germany; to retract the third, would be to encourage my adversaries in their struggle against the truth.' The official of Trèves urged him not to refuse all retractation. 'If Arius,' he said, 'had retracted certain errors, it would not have been necessary to burn his good books with his bad ones: they would find means to save his works, if he consented to expunge what had been condemned by the Council of Constance.' We see that Germany willingly subordinated the

infallibility of the Pope to that of councils. But
Luther believed in neither the one nor the other.
He answered, ' A council also may err.' And, upon
this being denied by the official, he offered to prove
that councils might err, and had erred. They did
not wish to begin that debate. The official demanded, for the last time, of Luther, if he was willing to maintain all that was in his books, or to
retract their contents, wholly or partially; sternly
declaring to him, that if he declined all retractation,
the Empire would know well how to treat an
obstinate heretic. Luther had expected, and was
prepared for, a discussion, a refutation; but when
he saw that the sole question lay between his condemning himself or being condemned, his noble
heart became only the more determined. He replied, calmly, ' If I am not convicted of error by
the text of the Holy Scriptures, I cannot, and I
will not retract: my conscience is bound by the
word of God. By that I hold; I cannot do otherwise. May God help me. Amen.'

The spectacle of that noble attitude thrilled
through the heart of all Germany. She felt that
she had a worthy representative in her apostle.
Her warriors admired his courage. When he entered the hall of the Diet, the veteran Freundsberg
clapped him on the shoulder in token of sympathy.
During the sitting, the brave Eric of Brunswick,

seeing him stifled by the heat, brought him beer in
a silver cup.   When he went out, he heard a voice
exclaiming, 'Blessed be the mother who bore thee!'
The princes visited and conversed familiarly with
him in his retirement.   Elsewhere, the opposition
assumed a more menacing aspect.   Billets were
found in the Emperor's apartments bearing this
inscription: 'Woe to the country whose king is a
child.'   Placards on the walls of the town, announced
to the Romanists that 400 knights were leagued
against them for the defence of oppressed honour
and law, and the just cause of Luther.   'I write
badly, but I act with vigour.   I have 8000 men at
my back!   *Bundschuh! Bundschuh! . . . .*'   That
formidable war-cry of the Swabian peasants was
recalled.   Resounding at that place, at that moment, it seemed to announce the alliance of the
knights and of the peasantry in favour of reform,—
an alliance often attempted, never realized.   The
courtiers felt themselves ill at ease in the midst of
a population so violently excited.   The wisest
among them still wished to attempt a compromise.
Also, when the Emperor proposed directly to the
Diet to treat Luther as a convicted heretic, the Diet
demanded a delay of some days.   These were employed in bringing all means to bear upon Luther.
They entreated him to retract at least his opinions
upon councils, and to accept the Emperor and the

Diet as judges of his doctrine. To the first proposal he answered, 'Yes, Huss has been unjustly condemned;' to the second, 'I cannot accept men for judges of the word of God.' Nothing could shake his resolution, and he departed, leaving the Diet in the most violent agitation.

A decision, however, remained to be taken. The Diet did not seem inclined to adhere to its former resolution. Many regretted it: the presence and the courage of Luther had excited vivid sympathy, and the unmistakeable expression of public opinion weighed upon the minds of a great number of the members of the Diet. The result of the definitive vote was, at any rate, doubtful. To turn it against Luther, his enemies had recourse to the means recommended by Aleander, *cunning and promptitude.*

For a long time there had been no dispute about anything. The Diet had finished its labours, and many of its members had gone away. On the 25th of May, the Emperor repaired to the hall of meeting, to go through the formality of the ratification of his decisions, and requested the Diet to protract its sittings for three days longer, in order to dispose of some affairs still pending. According to custom, the assembly escorted the Emperor, on his going out, as far as the episcopal palace, where he lodged. The Elector of Saxony and the Elector Palatine had already departed; the other four Electors were present. At the palace they found the papal nuncios, who delivered to them briefs addressed to them. Whilst they were discussing this extraordinary proceeding, the Emperor informed them that he had caused an edict to be drawn up with regard to Luther, in conformity with their previous decision, and ordered it to be read forthwith to the members of the Diet who were present. Either from being thus taken by surprise, or from conviction, no one made any objection; and the Elector of Brandenburg admitted that the edict was really agreeable to the previously expressed opinion of the Diet. Aleander lost no time in drawing up the act. That very day he made two copies, one in Latin and the other in German; and next day—a Sunday—he followed the Emperor even to the church, in order more speedily to obtain his signature. In short, to give a last specimen of his machinations: the edict was drawn up on the 26th of May; Aleander found it useful to antedate it on the 8th May, a day on which the Diet still consisted of a sufficient number of members.

Such is that famous legislative act, not submitted to the assembled Diet, not deliberated upon, not voted, but extorted by surprise from some members brought together by chance, many of whom would unquestionably have repudiated it if they had been able to consult together. ' Happy surprise,' piously exclaims a Roman Catholic writer, ' which has prevented the princes from perjuring themselves!'[1]

The edict was as violent as possible. Luther was put under the ban of the Empire, as a member cut off from the church of God; and all his adherents, protectors, and friends were included in the same sentence. His writings, and those of his partisans, were to be burnt; and in order to prevent any more copies from appearing, the censorship was established on all printed works.

This edict, however, did not arrest the progress of the Reformation; it did not deprive Luther of a single partisan: on the contrary, the public conscience revolted against such violence, and set itself, throughout all Germany, to oppose its execution. The circulation of the works of Luther and his friends went on increasing more and more, in spite of the censorship, in spite of the flames. One argument which is incessantly reappearing under the pen of these writers, and which seems to have produced the most powerful effect, is this: ' Why have they not refuted Luther at Worms?' It was found impossible to persuade the strong sense of justice in the nation, to accept a condemnation as a substitute for a refutation. A swarm of pam-

[1] C. Riffel, Christliche Kirchengeschichte der neusten Zeit, t. i. p. 214.

phlets was circulated throughout the country : but
the risk was great; and all the authors remained
anonymous. Hutten alone dared to sign his *brochure.*
It assailed no less a person than Aleander himself,
the author of the edict and the papal legate, and
inflicted on him the severe chastisement of indignant
patriotism and virtue.[1]

XXIII.

HUTTEN had not waited until this time,
in order to stir still more profoundly
public opinion, already so strongly excited. Since the opening of the Diet, he had
published four new dialogues : the *Bull,* the *First
Monitor,* the *Second Monitor,* the *Brigands.* The
Second Monitor and the *Brigands* are the most important of these writings : there are none which
throw more light on the projects of Hutten and his
friends. The speakers of the *Monitor* are the
Monitor and Sickingen.

The Monitor warns Sickingen of the evil reports
which are spread abroad with regard to him. They

---

[1] The greater part of this chapter is translated from Ranke's History
of Germany at the time of the Reformation, one of those books which
deserve to be better known in France.

suspect him of heresy, because he protects Luther and entertains Hutten; they fear that he is preparing some enterprise against the Pope, the bishops, and the clergy: 'It is a dangerous game; remember the proverb: No one has been the better for attacking the priests!'

Sickingen.—'That proverb has often lied. For proof of which, I need only refer to John Ziska, the invincible chief of the Hussites, in that long war against the priests. Has he not the renown of a great captain? Has he not the glory of having delivered his country from tyranny, purged Bohemia from these lazy priests and monks, and restored their goods in part to the heirs of the too generous donors? Has he not freed his country from the exactions of the Popes, and avenged the death of Huss, that holy man assassinated by the priests? And is it not well known that, in all his great undertakings, he never consulted his own advantage,—that he thought only of his native country and of religion? Besides, after having been fortunate in all his enterprises, he died amidst the grief and tears of his fellow-countrymen.'

The *Monitor.*—'It would really seem as if you were about to follow his example.'

Sickingen.—'And why not? If the clergy will not listen to our counsels, nor to our brotherly rebukes, we must at last have recourse to force.'

The *Monitor.*—' But supposing that the Emperor forbids you ?'

Sickingen.—' I shall not the less persist in my design. I act like those who, before constructing an edifice, calculate for a long time what it will cost, but who, the plan once determined on, carry it out to the end. Assuredly, I shall pay no attention to what perfidious or ignorant councillors now advise the Emperor, but to what he will approve of hereafter, when he will be older, and entertain more mature views. If our young Emperor had a burning fever, and asked me to give him cold water, should I give it to him ? I am too faithful and devoted a servant to do anything that could hurt him : to refuse to obey, is often the truest obedience. It would be best that the Emperor should not intermeddle with religious affairs. If, according to the selfish counsel of priests, he had not interfered with the natural course of events, the knowledge of Gospel doctrine, spread abroad by Luther, would have gradually improved mankind, have restored the imperial dignity, and driven the perverse and pernicious Romanists from the whole of Germany. His resolutions are in the hand of God. But, for my part, I shall always seek to serve rather than to flatter him. If he commanded me to do something against my conscience, I would publicly refuse obedience ; for we must obey God rather than man, especially when the matter relates to religion. If, then, I see that there is no hope from the Emperor, I shall attempt the enterprise at my own risk and peril, whatever may be the result.'

The *Monitor*.—' And towards that noble undertaking, you have a warm counsellor in your friend Ulrich von Hutten. He cannot endure any delay, and takes all the trouble in the world to draw down the tempest upon the heads of his enemies.'

Sickingen.—' Yes, assuredly : his services are precious to me ; he has the spirit necessary for such undertakings.'

XXIV.

WHAT, then, was the support upon which the two friends relied ? The Emperor was led away by the exigencies of his political position, and by the impatient promptings of his ambition ; the princes were indifferent, timid, or gained over by the court of Rome. What then remained ? Two great forces : the nobility and the people, especially the people of the cities ; for, at that epoch, scarcely even the bravest dared to contemplate the mighty mass of the rural population, so violently agitated by the breath of the Reformation. The important question was, to ascertain if a combination could be effected between the two, in some degree, regular forces of lay society, divided by so many prejudices, and by so many just grounds of complaint. This was one of the subjects which most profoundly occupied the mind of Hutten. The first attempt which he made to bring about so necessary a reconciliation, was the dialogue which had for its title the _Brigands_. The speakers are Hutten, Sickingen, and an agent of the great house of the Fuggers (33) at Augsburg. Hutten finds fault with the merchant, because he has termed the knights brigands. Sickingen interposes, calming his fiery friend, and thus addressing himself to the merchant:

'So far as concerns myself, I have no need of justification. Germany knows it, and history has taken note of it. I have never done harm to any man without declaring war against him.—The _Merchant:_ But by what right do you declare war? That reason does not excuse you.—_Sickingen:_ How! do you say that we have no right to make war after declaring it?—The _Merchant:_ No! not without the permission of the princes.—_Sickingen:_ I shall then ask you: must we preserve the nobility? —The _Merchant:_ Yes, I think so.—_Sickingen:_ Are the princes alone noble?—The _Merchant:_ No, assuredly. I reckon also among the nobility the counts, and even the simple knights, such as you are, so far as you act honourably ; for it has for a long time been my opinion, that nobility consists only in acting honourably.—*Sickingen :* You are right. I also think that honour and virtue are not hereditary ; and that whoever has been guilty of a shameful action, ought to be blotted out from the ranks of the nobility, even were he a prince. Not to imitate the glorious ancestors who have conquered nobility, is to lose it. I utterly despise all the pretended nobles, who have many quarterings, but few personal services—many ancestral pictures, and no crown around their own foreheads. I shall never consider as my equal, were he my nearest relation, a man with a stain on his life. But what do you term virtue in the nobility ?—The *Merchant :* Valour is commonly considered to be so.—*Sickingen :* You mean warlike virtue ; but what, in your opinion, is warlike virtue ?—The *Merchant :* Valour in the service of the right cause.—*Sickingen :* Very good ; and I draw this conclusion : all men are equal by nature ; but the most virtuous are the most noble. You will also grant me, that a man is so much the more noble, just in proportion as he more warmly defends the right. And lastly, you will agree that if the defence of the right belongs more especially to princes, it also belongs to nobles, since it is by that, according to your own statement, that they are noble.—The *Merchant*: Agreed, but on condition that you fight only under the orders of the princes.—*Sickingen*: But if they never order, if they are all absorbed in their private interests, indifferent to the general well-being, shall we not then make war ourselves?—The *Merchant*: It must be admitted that, under these circumstances, you possess the right to do so.—*Sickingen*: And if, when some one wishes to do you wrong, I avert that peril without awaiting the order of the princes, shall I not be acting rightly?—The *Merchant*: That would only be just.—*Sickingen*: You see, then, how far it would be doing us wrong, to deprive us of the only thing by which we are noble,—I mean the power of defending the right by arms. Because therein is our law and our duty: to succour the unfortunate, to raise up the oppressed, to avenge those who have been unjustly injured, to make head against the wicked, to protect widows and orphans. We do not blush to rank behind the princes; and we serve them faithfully, when we have voluntarily agreed to serve them. Beyond that, we recognise no other lord than the Emperor: in him we see the defender of the public liberty. But if the Emperor himself ordered us to do something contrary to right and justice, it would be our duty to refuse him obedience. He would himself tell you, if you could ask him, that he has not the right to order anything unjust, or to oppose anything just; and if the Emperor possesses not that right, how should the princes possess it?'

I doubt whether this somewhat sophistical apology converted the merchant. How very different were the facts of the case from that ideal of nobility, which the knight depicts in such magnificent language! The claim of the nobles to maintain their turbulent anarchy, explains the backwardness of the citizens of the great towns in this first episode of the long war for liberty of conscience. But it is the biographer's duty to combine all the traits which form the picture, and not to remove men from the midst of the age in which they lived and acted, in order to give them the ideas and the passions of another time.

Sickingen at length assumes the offensive. 'The great robbers are not those whom they hang on a gibbet: they are the priests and the monks, the chancellors and the doctors, the great merchants, especially the Fuggers.'—The *Merchant:* 'How? We thieves! We, who so thoroughly detest the knights on account of their brigandage!'—*Sickingen:* 'Yes, assuredly; you do not steal by open force, but by secret and underhand practices. Have not your masters, the Fuggers, by all means, just

I

and unjust, excluded the other merchants from
commerce with the Indies, in order that they alone
may be enriched by the importation of commodi-
ties equally injurious to the health and the morals
of the country? Is it not the wish of all good
citizens to see this public plague driven out? Or
will you venture to maintain that it is not theft
to inundate Germany with money under the just
weight, to monopolize the traffic with the Indies,
to add to it the traffic in papal dispensations, in
indulgences, in benefices,—to pour forth upon Germany all these drugs, and to receive in exchange
for them solid crowns?'

'But still more dangerous robbers are the doctors
and the chancellors of the princes, all these Rabulists (34), who, of late years, have pounced upon
our native country. Old men often recall the happy
time when that leprosy was unknown; and now
they are everywhere, they steal everywhere—in the
courts of the princes, in the senates and assem-
blies of the towns, in every meeting, public or
private, in peace, in war! And as to those who pre-
side in the tribunals! They are always seeking the
right and never finding it; they mould the laws
like soft wax, and turn them to their own profit:
between their venal hands the unjust becomes the
just. They do more harm to Germany than the
most disastrous war; and it would be better to cut

short our processes by arms than by their false and contradictory science. What happiness, if we could one day see all these doctors chased away, and all their books burnt!'

'Let us, however, be just: there are robbers still more pernicious in our unhappy country; such are the bishops, the canons, and the monks. Not content with having appropriated the richest and most beautiful part of Germany, with being gorged with wealth which they waste in criminal wars and in the most shameful pleasures, they corrupt the intellect and the heart of the people by superstition and by their evil example, abhor the science which would open the eyes of the nation, and render still more intolerable the yoke of the Popes, whose creatures they are. Have they not the audacity to maintain that the Vicar of Christ may change, extend, and limit the doctrine of the Saviour; condemn the most virtuous men; sanctify the most wicked; do, or omit to do, whatever he chooses, without any daring to complain! When we shall have broken the chains of the Romish tyranny, forced the priests to perform their duties, applied to the public use the revenues of the bishops, the canons and the monks, and the treasures of the churches, and abolished all the religious orders, then only will Germany be free and happy. But the princes are the obstacle in the way of this result, because they have their relations in the bishoprics, and fear to see them thrown on their hands.'

The *Merchant*: 'Therefore it is that such a noble and useful enterprise cannot be conducted to a successful issue.' *Hutten*: 'It is so much the more necessary that the knights should make the most favourable arrangement that they can with the cities, and should conclude an alliance with them. The cities are rich and powerful, and full of ardour for liberty. With their concurrence we can commence the war, the most just of wars, against our tyrants; for, if we have always considered it a duty to combat every description of tyranny, how much more ought we to rebel against those tyrants who attack not only our property, but also our faith and our religion, and who snatch from us the truth, and wish to destroy us body and soul! For my own part, what I desire is, that this war should begin to-day rather than to-morrow.'

And Sickingen calmly replies: 'Assuredly I shall second you with all my power when the moment shall have come. But you are in too great a hurry: if we yielded to your impatience, we should be crushed at the commencement of our undertaking. Besides, you have no cause to fear that this war will be too long delayed. By Luther and by you, Germany has been awakened from the profound sleep in which she was wrapped. The hour approaches which will be the most favourable for this great work.'

XXV.

HAVE given the greater part of this dialogue, because it explains the sentiments of the two friends, their projects, and the assistance upon which they believed that they might rely.   Their enterprise failed; and the triumph of religious liberty came from a quarter from which no one expected it.   The Reformation had made especial progress in the country, in the cities, and among the lower ranks of the nobility : the princes were hostile or indifferent to it.   Besides placing their younger sons in the best bishoprics, they found the court of Rome very complaisant in granting all the concessions which they coveted : history informs us that the first secularizations of church property were made without opposition on the part of the Pope, in the most Catholic countries,—in Bavaria, for example, and in the hereditary estates of Austria.   The princes were also well aware of the fact, that, at the root of the Reformation, in its early period, there was a mighty movement of national unity, entirely opposed to the constitution of principalities, and to the estab-

lishment of that oligarchical government which, for
more than a century, the Electors had not ceased
to aim at.   What was necessary to change all this?
Two things : the ruin of the lesser nobility by the
defeat of Sickingen ; and the determination of the
Emperor to side with the Pope, to refuse the support which the religious revolution offered him,
and to throw himself, the representative of national
unity, into the arms of the foreign oppressor.   At
this time, some of the princes declared themselves
in favour of the Reformation ; and if, in so doing,
they followed the impulse of their consciences, it is
not the less certain that, for them, the Reformation
was also a political instrument which led them to
the goal at which they aimed.   But none then fore-
boded the impending revolution of the wheel of fortune.   Hutten, who was always an enemy to political
selfishness, and Sickingen, the last and most illustrious representative of the lesser nobility against the
sovereignty of the princes, foresaw it less than any.

It would seem that, after the edict of Worms, they
ought to have lost all hope of obtaining the assistance of the Emperor.   His support was, however,
so necessary, and the idea of which he was the in-
carnation was so rooted in their hearts, that they
unceasingly returned to it.   For a moment, they
might yet believe that it would be possible to gain
him over to their cause.

Charles V., after having sacrificed Luther to the Pope, in order to make an enemy the more to Francis I., wished to make use of the talents of Sickingen, the energy of Hutten, and their influence over the nobility, for the same purpose. He sent to them, at the castle of Ebernburg, his confessor, Glapio. Glapio was really a very enlightened man, and as thoroughly convinced as any one could be, of the necessity of applying a remedy to the diseases of the church. It is said that he had menaced Charles with the wrath of Heaven if he did not correct them; but when he saw the tendency of Luther's doctrines, he became one of his most vehement persecutors. It may well be believed, however, that he showed himself in quite another light to the two friends. 'Never,' says Hutten, 'was there a greater hypocrite; everything about him was deception—the expression, the eyes, the mouth, the speech, and the gestures. He suited himself to all situations, and changed according to circumstances. "It is certain," said he to us, "that Luther has opened the gate through which all Christians have arrived at the true knowledge of the holy Scriptures." And when I demanded of him what fault he had committed that could be put in competition with such a benefit, he replied, " In truth I see none." And, notwithstanding, he has insisted more vehemently than any one, that Luther should be condemned without being allowed an opportunity of justifying himself, without even a hearing.'

It is improbable that this singular ambassador would have gained over the two friends, if they had not seen, in the overtures made by the Emperor, a last chance of attaching him to their party. Sickingen raised an army of 3000 cavalry and 12,000 infantry. He wished, by a bold march, to penetrate into the heart of France; but the Count of Nassau, to whom he held a subordinate command, insisted upon besieging Mézières. There, Bayard and Sickingen, the two last representatives of the chivalry of France and Germany, worthy of each other's rivalry and of each other's friendship, found themselves opposed. The Imperialists were repulsed. Sickingen lost in this expedition the sum he had expended in raising his army, and the hope of attaching the Emperor by gratitude for his services.

The desire of wiping out the stain given to his reputation by this defeat, and perhaps also of recruiting his exhausted finances, added to the religious motives which impelled Sickingen to commence the war against the priests; because it must be admitted that this hero loved money, and liked to amass it. But the aid of the Emperor hopelessly gone, it became only the more necessary to combine all the elements of opposition. The Rhenish knights, assembled at Landau on the summons of

Hutten and Sickingen, formed a league for the defence of their interests, and undoubtedly, also, for those of the Reformation: they elected Sickingen as their chief. At the same time, a number of writings were circulated among the people, in order to rouse them to action. Among these, there is one of which Hutten appears to be the author, and which deserves to occupy our attention. It is still in the form of a dialogue, entitled the *New Karsthans*, the supplement to another *Karsthans*, written in the Alsacian dialect by an unknown author. It appears, however, that this Karsthans was a real and a popular personage, a peasant who traversed the countries bordering on the Rhine, preaching the doctrines of Luther.

The speakers in the *New Karsthans* are Sickingen and the peasant. The knight asks the latter why he has an air of so much anxiety. ' How can I be gay with these priests, who harass us in every way? I no longer know what to do; and if this lasts, I shall forget myself grossly; for truly their conduct passes a joke.' Sickingen exhorts him to take courage, and tells him that the face of affairs may, before long, be entirely changed. But the peasant has not much hope. Then follows a dialogue, in which the speakers, by turns, expose the exactions of the priests, their avarice, their luxury, their whole conduct, so opposed to the doc-

trines of Christ. Karsthans frequently interrupts
himself in order to exclaim: 'Ah! then it will
truly be necessary that afflictions come!' Both
are agreed that the Pope is Antichrist, that the
nobility and the people are ruined by the priests,
and that this state of things cannot last. It will
therefore be necessary to employ force if the priests
will not listen to reason. 'He was no fool, that
Ziska,' says the peasant, 'when he demolished the
churches; if he had left them standing, his predic-
tion to the Bohemians would assuredly have been
verified. He said to them: " Leave the nests, and
in ten years you will find the birds" (35). I cannot
help admiring him for having chased away and
extirpated all the monks, these insatiable slug-
gards, from whom come all our woes.' Sickingen
is also of opinion that the chapters, convents, and
perpetual foundations, must be suppressed.—*Karsthans:* 'That would have happened a long time
ago to the whole brood, if the nobility had been
willing; but you were not willing.'—At the end of
the dialogue are thirty articles, gages of the alliance
solemnly sworn between Karsthans and the knights
Hulfreich and Heintz. They are of extreme audacity, and we afterwards find them among the documents of the peasants, in their great insurrection.

I can only mention a poem addressed to the free
towns, to induce them to combine with the lesser

nobility against the usurpations and violence of the princes, and a letter of Hutten to the town of Worms, which we may consider as an overture made by Sickingen to his oldest enemies. At that critical moment, the two knights perhaps felt, in the same degree, the desire of strengthening their cause by gaining new allies, and that of reconciling themselves with their former enemies. Men do not begin so mighty an enterprise without bethinking them of the chance of death.

After the publication of these last mentioned writings, the war of religion commenced, to be no more interrupted, except by truces, until 1648. Who can deny the oceans of blood which that age-long war cost Germany and the whole of Europe? (36). But it is the fatality of history that the past may not give way to the future without violence. Must the truth therefore hide her face, must the future be kept back, must progress be arrested? May the blood shed fall upon the heads of those who have not had the wisdom to withdraw in time! And we who, after having given so many examples to the world, are to-day reduced to receive them, may that solemn, heroic strife confirm us in our faith! The dead alone sleep in their tombs; the living live; and to live is to strive, and, alas! to suffer. Happy those who, in times of civil strife, and of wars for conscience' sake, strive and suffer for the truth! The champions of the future, happy, even in their sufferings!

XXVI.

A VARIETY of causes contributed to the failure of the first war of the Reformation. The two friends and their ardent associates at Ebernburg had calculated everything, except time, which matures the thoughts of men, and ripens their fruits. And then, too, it must be confessed, that their foundation was not laid on firm ground. To unite the reformation of religion with the restoration of the nobility, was to seek to attach the future to the past, the living to the dead. In this way, the Reformation made itself suspected by the cities and by the peasantry, as well as odious to the princes. It aspired to give an impulse to the world along the path of progress, and itself retrograded several centuries. Political and religious reformation assuredly ought not to be separated; but it was the misfortune of that early period, that the Reformation allied itself to a policy contradictory to its instincts, and to the wants of the age. Hutten wished to give a mighty impulse to liberty, as all his writings testify. Emancipated from the prejudices of the nobility, he boasts of the liberal spirit of the towns, and praises it on every occasion. He even stretches out the hand of friendship to the passion for independence, which smouldered among the peasantry. And he would not have given utterance to that cruel saying of Luther: 'Better that all the peasants should perish, than that the princes and the magistrates should suffer any injury; for the peasants have taken up the sword against the will of God!' But his friends and allies had not shaken off their ancient hatreds and their hereditary pride: what they especially wished, was the re-establishment of the feudal anarchy crushed by the sovereignty of the princes; and it was this that the peasantry (37) and the citizens of the great towns detested above everything. From that unhappy alliance resulted the ruin of the plans so long organized. Besides, Luther, who possessed political tact in a high degree, refused to combine with his friends. 'The Word has conquered the world,' he exclaimed; 'the Word shall save it.' Upon which Hutten replied, 'Our paths are different: as for me, I am influenced by purely human considerations; while you, more perfect, place everything in the hands of God!'

War resolved upon, Sickingen did not long hesitate as to which enemy he should first attack. He had an old quarrel to settle with the Archbishop of Trêves, and he counted on finding allies among the inhabitants of the country. It was against him that he directed his forces. To mark clearly the aim and the spirit of his enterprise, he gave as the watchword to his army: *Let the will of the Lord be done!* And he addressed the following manifesto to the troops of the Archbishop: 'Dear brethren and neighbours, wherefore do you march against me? Is not my cause yours? I come to deliver you from the antichristian yoke of priests, to bring you the light of the Gospel, and to make you enjoy Christian liberty, and yet you fight against me! Like men attacked by a mortal malady, who will not submit to be cured! Reflect that you are fighting against Christ and His Gospel, and not against me! For Christ and His Gospel I brave death! May the will of the Lord be done!'

Sickingen encountered a resistance which he did not anticipate; and the succours which ought to have arrived from Clèves, Cologne, and Brunswick, were crushed before they could join him. At the same time, he learned that the Count Palatine and the Elector of Hesse, were advancing to give him battle under the very walls of Trêves. He was compelled to raise the siege. The princes hotly pursued him, and successively destroyed all the castles of his partisans.

As to Sickingen, firmly resolved to prosecute the

war, but feeling all its perils, he separated himself
from those of his friends who were most compromised, especially from those who, like Hutten and
Œcolampadius, had everything to fear, and whose
genius was necessary to the cause. Then he shut
himself up in the castle of Landstuhl, which was considered impregnable, and in which he hoped to be
able to sustain a long siege, and wait the coming of
the promised reinforcements. But the besiegers'
cannon soon beat down the walls, and battered the
castle into a mass of ruins. Sickingen himself was
mortally wounded by the fall of a fragment of wall.
He made up his mind to capitulate, demanding,
according to custom, that he should be allowed to
go forth free. The princes refused. 'I shall not be
their prisoner long,' he exclaimed, and surrendered
at discretion. He had scarcely sufficient strength
remaining to sign the capitulation. The princes
found him dying, stretched under a vault, sole relic
of the castle. The Archbishop of Trêves said to
him, 'Wherefore, Franz, have you attacked me
and my poor people?' Sickingen replied, 'I have
an account to render to a more powerful Lord than
you.' His chaplain asked if he wished to confess himself. He replied, 'I have confessed myself to God in
my conscience.' The chaplain recited the prayers
for the dying, and raised the host. The princes
uncovered themselves, and fell upon their knees.

At that moment the hero expired. The princes repeated a *Pater* for his soul.[1]

<hr />

XXVII.

ON leaving Sickingen, Hutten and Œcolampadius directed their steps towards Switzerland. Without resources, on account of his having given up his fortune to his family, without a country, without a secure refuge, Hutten nevertheless refused a pension of 400 crowns offered him by Francis I., with the right of choosing his place of residence. His patriotism recoiled, even in that distress, from the idea of becoming a pensioner on the bounty of the Emperor's enemy.

Hutten was warmly welcomed at Basle. The members of the Council, the whole population, thronged around the proscribed unfortunate. Erasmus alone, his oldest friend, he whom Hutten had once so highly praised, and who formerly had been so proud of his praises, kept aloof from him. He begged Hutten· not to visit him, if it was not absolutely necessary for him to do so. And subsequently, after the death of Hutten, he had the

[1] *Ranke*, following the Chronicle of Flersheim.

effrontery to write to Melancthon, 'that he had kept at a distance from Hutten, because he only sought a nest in which to die;' so little is sometimes the heart in the greatest intellects!

The Bishop and his adherents strongly insisted upon the removal of Hutten. The Senate, not daring to resist, but not wishing to mix themselves up with persecutions which they really detested, requested Hutten to leave the town for the sake of the public peace, and for his own personal safety. He repaired to Mulhausen. The magistrates and the citizens had already decided upon the establishment of the Reformation; and on the 12th March 1523, he had the pleasure of assisting in the solemn suppression of the papal power in that city. The sympathy of which he was the object softened the bitterness of his patriotic griefs, and made him forget the malady, which travelling, the uncertainty of his position, and so many misfortunes, had rendered more severe than ever, when he received a letter written by Erasmus, containing fresh insults against himself, mingled with perfidious attacks upon the principal Reformers. This new cowardice roused all his rage; and in a violent pamphlet, whose violence, however, was well deserved, he chastised the weaknesses and compromises of conscience, of the man who wished at once to preserve the tranquillity of his private life,

K

and to sow the seeds of war throughout the world by his writings!

The Reformation, however, was not established at Mulhausen without opposition, and without reaction. A disturbance, excited by the priests, compelled Hutten to seek another asylum. He took refuge at Zurich, beside Zwingli, the great Reformer. 'Is this,' writes the latter to Pirckheimer, ' your terrible Hutten, that destroyer, that conqueror! He who behaves with such sweetness towards his friends, towards little children, towards the humblest of men! How can we believe that a tongue so amiable has raised up such a tempest!'

Hutten's strength was now far spent, and he already felt the approach of death. On the 12th May 1524, he writes to his friend Eoban Hess, at Erfurth: 'Will destiny never cease to pursue me so cruelly! My only consolation is, that I have courage equal to my misfortunes. Germany, prostrate as she is, can no longer afford me an asylum: a voluntary exile has conducted me to Switzerland, and will perhaps conduct me still farther. . . . . I hope that God will one day reunite all the friends of the truth, now dispersed throughout the world, and that He will humble our enemies.' We love to cherish the belief, that this hope did not abandon the hero before his last hour, and that it sweetened for him the bitterness of death, far from his native country, far from all he held dear.

Zwingli had sent Hutten to the little island of Uffnau, to be under the care of the clergyman, who was well acquainted with medicine. There it was that he died, on the 29th August 1524, at the age of thirty-six, in the most complete destitution (38). He is buried in that green isle, at the extremity of the Lake of Zurich, at the feet of the mighty Alps. No monument marks the place where a hero reposes; and by an ironical caprice of destiny, the sepulchre of the vehement enemy of monasticism now belongs to the Convent of Einsiedeln. The tears of his friends were not wanting to his memory. Crotus Rubianus, Melancthon, Hess especially, bade him, with tender emotion, an eternal adieu. 'None was a greater enemy of the wicked; none a more devoted friend of the good.' These words of a man who knew him thoroughly,[1] admirably sum up the life of one of the noblest champions of liberty!

[1] *Eoban Hess*, Letter to Draco.

NOTES

BY

THE TRANSLATOR.

TRANSLATOR'S NOTES.

Note 1, page 18.

Crotus Rubianus was the bosom friend of Hutten from childhood till death. He was an accomplished scholar, and a fine vein of satire distinguished his genius. In his discussions on philosophy and literature, Sir William Hamilton has proved, with a rare affluence of learning and acuteness of argument, that Crotus Rubianus and Hermannus Buschius had a share, along with Hutten, in the composition of the *Epistolæ Obscurorum virorum*.

Note 2, page 18.

Eitelwolf von Stein, who so early appreciated the dawning genius of Hutten, was a man of great intelligence and ability, as well as an excellent classical scholar. He was born in Swabia in 1466, and was the first German knight who respected and cultivated the arts of peace, and who attempted to dispel the prejudices of the caste to which he belonged, which led them to regard war as the only occupation befitting men of noble birth, and to look upon all kinds of study with contempt and aversion. Eitelwolf had the principal share in founding the High School of Mayence, which he endeavoured to make the first seminary of its kind in Germany. He looked forward to the perfecting of this school as the chief occupation of his declining years, when he should have withdrawn from the cares of business, and the toils of war. But his premature death, in 1515, prevented this expectation from being ever realized. At the time of his death, he occupied the important offices of Governor and Hof-Marshall of the town of Mayence. Besides some letters, he published a work entitled, '*De laudibus heroum et virorum illustrium.*'

Note 3, page 20.

Ragius Æsticampianus had the honour of being expelled from the University of Leipsic for his attachment to the new learning, and his opposition to the effete scholasticism. The universities of Germany in general, were the bitterest persecutors of the revivers of classical learning. Like most corporations, they had a strong dislike to innovation.

Note 4, page 23.

Bilibald Pirckheimer, a celebrated historian and philologist, called by the Protestants of Germany

the Xenophon of Nuremberg, was born in that city
of a patrician family in 1470. His father was
councillor to the Bishop of Eichstædt; and at
eighteen the young Pirckheimer joined the troops
of the Bishop, in order to acquire a knowledge of
military discipline. He soon, however, left the
army and went to Italy, where he studied civil law
at Padua and Pisa, at the same time acquiring a
knowledge of Greek, mathematics, theology, and
medicine. He spent seven years in Italy, and then
returned to Nuremberg, where he became a member of the senate. He did not, however, definitively
abandon the military career, and took the command
of the contingent of troops furnished by the town of
Nuremberg, to aid the Emperor Maximilian in his
war against the Swiss. At the close of the war, he
was created imperial councillor. He died at Nuremberg in 1530. Pirckheimer had formed, with
much care, a choice library of the best Greek and
Latin authors, which was afterwards acquired by
Lord Arundel, from whom it passed to the Duke of
Norfolk, and subsequently to the Royal Society of
London.

Note 5, page 27.

Budæus was born at Paris in 1467, the year of
the birth of Erasmus. He was the most learned
Frenchman of his time. By his advice the College

of France and the Royal Library were founded, and
his fortune and credit were constantly at the service
of the cause of learning.   He was the restorer of
Greek literature in France, and was taught Greek
by Hermotymus, who took refuge in France after
the taking of Constantinople by the Turks.   He
also received lessons from John Lascaris, a Greek
of illustrious family, who came to France in 1494.
On dismissing Hermotymus, Budæus presented
him with 500 golden crowns.   In 1497, the fame
of Budæus for learning recommended him to Charles
VIII., who appointed him one of his secretaries.
On the death of that monarch, he retired from court,
and devoted himself to his favourite studies.   He
published various translations from the Greek and
Latin classics.   But his Treatise *De Asse* is his most
famous work.   No learned work ever obtained such
immense and sustained success.   A vast number of
editions and abridgments of it have been published,
and not long ago a copy of it on vellum sold for
L.60.   In August 1522, Budæus was elected by
the municipal corporation of Paris to the office of
prévôt des marchands ; and recently—in 1842—the
municipality of Paris erected a statue to his memory among those of their first magistrates.   The
works of Budæus were collected and published, in
four volumes folio, at Basle in 1557.   It has been
affirmed by some that Budæus had a tendency to-

wards the doctrines of Calvin; and it is certain
that, after his death, his widow and the greater
part of his numerous family abjured Catholicism
and retired to Geneva.

Note 6, page 28.

Erasmus has wittily been termed ' l'homme de
repos à tout prix;' and Ranke says of him, 'his
air was so timorous that he looked as if a breath
would overthrow him, and he trembled at the very
name of death.' He was the complete type of
feebleness of character united to vastness of intellect. No one more clearly discerned, or more
powerfully described, the corruptions of Rome, the
ignorance and depravity of the religious orders, the
luxury and fanaticism of the bishops and theologians, the utter rottenness of the whole existing
ecclesiastical fabric. Yet he was constantly seeking frivolous excuses to escape from the practical
consequences of his own principles and writings;
and his shuffling, vacillating conduct, in spite of his
splendid abilities, at length exposed him to the
contempt both of the adversaries and the defenders
of civil and religious liberty.

Note 7, page 31.

The Duke of Wurtemberg was connected with the
reigning family of Bavaria, and also with the Em-

peror himself; and he was permitted to compound for the cowardly murder which he had committed by a payment of 27,000 florins.

Note 8, page 36.

Franz von Sickingen was born, in 1481, in the castle of Sickingen, situated in what is now the Grand Duchy of Baden. His father was a gentleman of no very distinguished lineage, and was put to death by the Emperor Maximilian, on account of the troubles he had excited in the Empire. From his youth up Sickingen was a man of war; and the remarkable activity and ability which he displayed in making partisans, and in raising troops to avenge his father's death, made him, though but a simple knight, a formidable enemy to the Emperor. By force or by stratagem, he succeeded in making himself master of a number of strong places. The Duke of Lorraine, the town of Metz, and the Landgrave of Hesse, especially suffered from his attacks, and were at length obliged to pay him a sort of black mail. Sickingen was proud of his position as a free knight, relying only upon God, the Emperor, and his own good sword. He proclaimed himself a general redresser of wrongs; and his exploits in succouring the oppressed, and supporting the feeble against the strong, spread his reputation

throughout Germany, where he was regarded as a
sort of national hero. Yet there can be no doubt
that he was sometimes guilty of culpable excesses,
in the name of justice. He was often applied to by
those who had been wronged, and who were too
weak to right themselves; and in compelling a
powerful noble or an imperial city to pay a debt
unjustly withheld from a private person, he was
not always scrupulous about forms, or slow in the
employment of force. One of his great objects
seems to have been, to oppose and to humble the
despotism and pride of the princes and clergy; but
it is by no means certain that he did not entertain ulterior views, and aim at bringing about a
complete political revolution in Germany, which his
position in that warlike age as the acknowledged
flower of German chivalry, and the head and leader
of the lesser nobility of the Empire, might perhaps
have enabled him to accomplish. In the earlier
part of his adventurous career, Sickingen was presented to Francis I. as one well fitted to assist him
in his canvass for the Empire; and that ambitious
monarch loaded him with presents, and conferred on
him a pension of 1000 crowns. But Sickingen was
offended that Francis had not also taken him into
his confidence. 'The king,' he said to Fleuranges,
' but ill knows me, if he believes me more grateful
for favours than for confidence. I have penetrated

his designs, which you and he have endeavoured to conceal from me: he wishes to obtain the Empire: I have asked him for troops; he has believed that I asked them in order to carry out my own ends, whereas I asked them solely with the view of attaching to his party a greater number of German gentlemen. Warn him that he will never be well served but by simple gentlemen like myself; if he negotiates with the great Princes and the Electors, they will take his money and will betray him.' A circumstance soon afterwards occurred, which produced a total rupture between Francis and the great German partisan. A dispute had taken place between some German and Milanese merchants. Sickingen constituted himself the ally of the former, and seized effects belonging to the latter to the value of L.1000. On hearing of this act of summary justice, Francis demanded that Sickingen should restore the goods; and on the knight's sending a haughty refusal, he immediately stopped his pension. Upon this, Sickingen considered all his engagements to Francis cancelled, and from that period became one of his bitterest enemies; and his opposition contributed not a little to the failure of the efforts of the French king to obtain the imperial crown. Sickingen's subsequent invasion of France; the siege of Mezières, where the two model knights of France and Germany met face to face;

his ill-judged and disastrous war against the Archbishop of Trêves; and his death amidst the crumbling
ruins of his stronghold; are recounted with much
spirit and ability in the narrative of M. Chauffour-
Kestner. But we want in English a more detailed
biography of this remarkable man, who, next to Ulrich
von Hutten among the free knights of the German
Empire, most powerfully contributed to the revival of
letters and the reformation of religion,—a man who,
though belonging only to the lesser nobility, exercised
so powerful an influence on his own age, that some
of his enemies termed him the anti-emperor, and
others the anti-pope; whose friendship was courted,
and whose enmity was dreaded by all; who was the
type and model of German knighthood, and the
chosen leader of the lesser nobility in their war
against the princes; who repeatedly offered Luther
a safe and inviolable asylum, if he should be compelled to fly from the violence of his enemies; and
who received and protected Œcolampadius and
Hutten, until his own cause became desperate, and
then sent them away, lest lives so precious to the
Reformation should be involved in his destruction.
It is true, indeed, that the splendour of Sickingen's
character was somewhat dimmed by its faults. He
was occasionally rash and headstrong, high-handed
and heedless of law, as well as too much attached
to the right of private war, so inimical to all good

and settled government. But these were the faults
of the age in which he lived, and of the order to
which he belonged; and in spite of them, he would
have been well entitled to appropriate the proud
claim which Goethe has put in the mouth of Goetz
von Berlichingen, in that masterly drama which so
admirably depicts the state of Germany at the dawn
of the Reformation :—' Let them show me where I
have preferred my interest to my honour.   God
knows, my ambition has ever been to labour for my
neighbours as for myself, and to acquire the fame
of a gallant and irreproachable knight, rather than
princedoms or power; and God be praised! I have
gained the meed of my labour.'

Should the reception of the present sketch of the
life of Ulrich von Hutten be such as to justify him
in the attempt, the Translator hopes to supplement
it by a biography of Franz von Sickingen.

Note 9, page 38.

' The character of Reuchlin,' says Sir William
Hamilton, in his admirable article on the character
and authorship of the *Epistolæ Obscurorum virorum,*
' is one of the most remarkable in that remarkable
age.   It exhibits, in the highest perfection, a combination of qualities which are in general found in-
compatible.   At once a man of the world and of
books, he excelled equally in practice and specula-

tion; was a statesman and a philosopher, a jurist
and a divine. Nobles, and princes, and emperors
honoured him with their favour, and employed him
in their most difficult affairs; while the learned
throughout Europe looked up to him as the " *tri-
lingue miraculum*," the "*phœnix literarum*," the " *eru-
ditorum ἄλφα*." In Italy, native Romans listened
with pleasure to his Latin declamation; and he
compelled the jealous Greeks to acknowledge that
" Greece had overflown the Alps." Of his countrymen, he was the first to introduce the study of
ancient literature into the German universities; the
first who conquered the difficulties of the Greek
language; the first who opened the gates of the East,
unsealed the word of God, and unveiled the sanctuary of Hebrew wisdom. Agricola was the only
German of the fifteenth century who approached
him in depth of classical erudition; and it was not
till after the commencement of the sixteenth that
Erasmus rose to divide with him the admiration of
the learned. As an Oriental scholar, Reuchlin died
without a rival. Cardinal Fisher, who "almost
adored his name," made a pilgrimage from England
for the sole purpose of visiting the object of his worship; and that great divine candidly confesses to
Erasmus, that he regarded Reuchlin as "bearing
off from all men the palm of knowledge, especially
in what pertained to the hidden matters of religion

L

and philosophy."' Frederick Schlegel, in his Lectures on Modern History, speaks in equally high terms of this 'rare and profound spirit.' 'Reuchlin,' he says, 'one of the first scholars that Germany ever produced, and as much at home in Italy as in his native country, united all the literary culture, all the knowledge and learning, which either country, at the end of the fifteenth century, could supply. Not content with being the powerful critic and restorer of the then reviving Greek literature, he was, at the same time, for all Europe, the founder and creator of Oriental studies. Unlike later scholars and men of letters, however, these studies were not with him a mere matter of philology, of historical compilation, or of rhetorical brilliancy; he directed all his researches to the highest object of knowledge, that which the inquiring mind must ever consider its principal concern, namely, the knowledge of man, of nature, and of God.'

Note 10, page 45.

Ortuinus Gratius was a man of considerable learning, and held the important office of head of the College of Cologne. His own works are obsolete; but he has been preserved, like a fly in amber, by the biting satire of Hutten and his friends.

Jacob Hochstraten was prior of the Dominicans, and chief inquisitor at Cologne. *Arnold of Tungern* was Dean of the Theological Faculty at Cologne, and drew up and published in 1512 a pamphlet entitled, '*Articuli sive propositiones de Judaico favore nimis suspectæ ex libello teutonico Joannis Reuchlin.*'

Note 11, page 45.

' Never,' says Sir William Hamilton, ' were unconscious barbarism, self-glorious ignorance, intolerant stupidity, and sanctimonious immorality, so ludicrously delineated; never did delineation less betray the artifice of ridicule. The *Epistolæ Obscurorum Virorum* are at once the most cruel and the most natural of satires; and, as such, they were the most effective. They converted the tragedy of Reuchlin's persecution into a farce; annihilated in public consideration the enemies of intellectual improvement; determined a radical reform in the German universities; and even the friends of Luther, in Luther's lifetime, acknowledged that no other writing had contributed so powerfully to the downfall of the papal domination.'

Note 12, page 46.

In England cleverer men than the Dominican prior mistook the *Epistolæ Obscurorum Virorum* for a serious work, of which Sir William Hamilton relates the following curious anecdote :—' Erasmus would have wondered less at the stupidity of the sufferers, and more, perhaps, at the dexterity of the executioner, could he have foreseen that one of the most learned scholars of England, and the most learned of her bibliographers, should have actually *republished* these letters as a serious work; and that one of our wittiest satirists should have *reviewed* that publication, without even a suspicion of the lurking Momus. And, what is almost equally astonishing, the misprision has never been remarked. In 1710, there was printed in London the most elegant edition that has yet appeared of the *Epistolæ Obscurorum Virorum*, which the editor, Michael Maittaire, gravely represents as the production of their ostensible authors, and takes credit to himself for rescuing, as he imagines, from oblivion, so curious a specimen of conceited ignorance and unconscious absurdity. The edition he dedicates " *Isaaco Bickerstaff, Armigero, Magnæ Britanniæ Censori;*" and Steele, in a subsequent number of the *Tatler*, after acknowledging the compliment, thus notices the book itself: " The purpose of the work is signified in the dedication, in very elegant language, and fine raillery. It seems this is a collection of letters, which some profound blockheads, who lived before our times, have written in honour of each other, and for their mutual information in each other's absurdities (!). They are mostly of the German nation, whence, from time to time, inundations of writers have flowed, more pernicious to the learned world than the swarms of Goths and Vandals to the politic (!!). It is, methinks, wonderful that fellows could be awake, and utter such incoherent conceptions, and converse with great gravity like learned men, without the least taste of knowledge or good sense. It would have been an endless labour to have taken any other method of exposing such impertinences, than by an edition of their own works, where you see their follies, according to the ambition of such virtuosi, in a most correct edition" (!!!). And so forth. The monks are no marvel after this.'

Note 13, page 47.

Dr Strauss, in his excellent life of Hutten, published in 1858, also adverts to the impossibility of rendering the *Epistolæ Obscurorum Virorum* in a translation. 'Though we have honestly endeavoured,' he says, 'to give the reader an idea of the scope and contents, the form and design, of the *Letters of Obscure Men*, we must yet in conclusion make the disheartening confession, that we have undertaken what it is impossible properly to perform. . . . . No form in which the translator may handle the German or any other language can reproduce the impression of the original.'

Note 14, page 48.

The best authorities make Hutten the author of
the greater portion of the work, but also assign the
authorship of part of it to Crotus, and to Hermannus
Buschius, who was the literary opponent and personal foe of Ortuinus Gratius, to whom the *Epistolæ Obscurorum Virorum* are addressed, and who
is the principal victim of the satire.   Dr Friederich
Strauss gives Crotus Rubianus the credit of the
happy idea of parodying, in the fictitious letters of
the *Epistolæ Obscurorum Virorum*, the work which
Reuchlin had published in 1514, under the title of
*Epistolæ illustrium virorum ad Reuchlinum, virum
nostra ætate doctissimum,* as a sort of testimonial
in his favour from the most distinguished culti-
vators of classical learning throughout Europe.

Note 15, page 48.

This was very ungrateful of Erasmus, who is said
to have been cured of an imposthume in his face,
by the laughter produced on reading the *Epistolæ
Obscurorum Virorum.*

Note 16, page 55.

Hutten was naturally proud of this gallant ex-
ploit.   He celebrates it in six epigrams, and boasts
of it to the Emperor in the third of his philippics
against the Duke of Wurtemberg.

Note 17, page 55.

The diploma which conferred upon him that dignity, with all the privileges thereto attached, has been preserved: from this period Hutten assumes the title of *Poëta et Orator*. He is represented on the frontispiece of his writings as completely armed, and his brow girt with laurels; later in his career, when the war against Rome had commenced, his portraits depict him with his hand on the hilt of his sword, which is half drawn from its sheath. Dr Strauss makes the date of Hutten's coronation 12th July 1517, and states that he was decorated with the laurel crown by the hand of Maximilian himself.

Note 18, page 55.

Conrad Peutinger was the first German man of letters who devoted himself to the study and collection of antiquities. He was born at Augsburg, of a patrician family, in 1465. He studied law at Padua; and at Rome, was a pupil of the celebrated scholar Pomponius Lætus. Before leaving Italy, he became doctor both of the civil and canon law. On his return to his native town, he speedily distinguished himself both by the extent and variety of his learning, and by his capacity for business. He bestowed much time upon the study of inscriptions and antiques, and formed a precious collection of books and manuscripts, which he freely threw open to the public. He had the principal share in establishing a society for the purpose of printing the works of the best Greek and Latin authors. Peutinger was much esteemed by his fellow-citizens, and was frequently deputed by them to maintain their interests with the Emperor Maximilian, who was so much pleased with his talents and learning, that he appointed him one of his councillors. In 1519, he was sent to congratulate Charles V. on his accession to the Empire; and in 1521, he assisted at the Diet of Worms, when he succeeded in procuring a confirmation of the ancient statutes of Augsburg, and the additional privilege of coining money. He died in 1547, at the advanced age of eighty-two. One of Peutinger's principal claims to fame rests on the famous chart, known as the *Tabula Peutingeriana*. This interesting geographical monument—supposed by some authorities to have been executed at Constantinople in 393 by order of the Emperor Theodosius, and by others in 435—was discovered by Conrad Celtes in an ancient library at Spires. At his death, he bequeathed it to Peutinger, who believed it to be the Itinerary of Antoninus; and proposed to publish it for the benefit of lovers of antiquity, but did not find time to carry out his purpose. It was found in his library by Mark

Velser, forty years after his death, and printed in
1598. It has since been several times reproduced,
especially by Scheyb, in folio, in 1753, and by
another editor in 1809. The original is now in
the Library of Vienna.

Note 19, page 56.

Laurentius Valla was one of the most accomplished scholars of the early part of the fifteenth
century, and one of the most efficient and successful promoters of the revival of classical learning. He was born at Rome in 1406, where his
father was Consistorial Advocate to the Holy
See. He studied Latin under Leonardo d'Arezzo,
and also acquired a competent knowledge of the
Greek language; but it was as an elegant and
accomplished Latinist that he won his greenest
laurels. Like most of the learned men who took
a leading part in the great movement of the
Rénaissance, he led a stormy and troubled life,—
occupied in literary strifes, in attacking his enemies,
or in replying to their assaults. He first attacked
Bartolus, a famous jurist, who taught the civil law
at Pavia—whose followers Hutten frequently stig-
matizes under the title of Bartolists—principally
because the barbarous Latin employed by him and
his pupils offended the delicacy of his classical ear.
In the piquant pamphlet which he wrote against

him—which was the work of a single night—he designates Bartolus, Baldus, and Accursius as the *geese* who had succeeded to Scævola, Paulus, and Ulpian, the *swans* of jurisprudence. Valla distinguished himself as a teacher in many towns of Italy—in Pavia, Milan, Genoa, and Florence. From 1435 to 1442, he followed the fortunes of Alphonso of Arragon, in his wars for the conquest of the kingdom of Naples; and in 1440, he published the celebrated work mentioned in the text, under the title of '*Declamatio de falsò credita Constantini donatione.*' The pretended donation of Constantine was then loudly vaunted by the Holy See, and implicitly believed in France, Spain, Great Britain, and Germany. Valla, however, attacked the obscure author of this absurd invention, with the utmost violence and indignation; and, with consummate skill and marvellous erudition, brought forward an irresistible mass of evidence to demonstrate its futility and falsehood. But his presumption in thus attempting to sap the foundation on which rested the temporal power of the Holy See, drew down upon him its unsparing and dangerous enmity, and he was compelled to fly from Italy. He afterwards returned, however, and was well received at Naples by King Alphonso, his friend and patron. But he soon became involved in another ecclesiastical controversy. He ventured to impugn the

assertion of a popular preacher, that the Apostles'
Creed had been composed, clause by clause, by the
apostles—each apostle, beginning with Peter, successively enunciating a separate clause. The Inquisition would have seized him in its fatal grasp
for thus presuming to controvert the popular belief,
had it not been for the powerful protection of his
steady friend, King Alphonso. The work which
most contributed to the fame of Valla was his
treatise '*De Elegantia Linguæ Latinæ.*' It was the
favourite text-book during the whole of the sixteenth century; Erasmus always professed the
greatest admiration for it, and wrote an epitome
of it for his own use, which was afterwards published. Perhaps the most bitter of the many paper
wars in which Valla was engaged, was that which
he waged against Poggio Bracciolini, that famous
scholar and successful discoverer of ancient classical
manuscripts. It was disgraced by the virulence
of the abuse with which the enraged disputants
profusely bespattered each other. Valla died at
Naples in 1457, at the age of fifty-two.

Note 20, page 61.

It ought not to be forgotten, that Hutten's decisive attack upon the pretensions of the Papacy was
made some time before Luther took any determined
step in the same direction; and it is interesting to

observe how the writings of Hutten influenced a
genius as original and fearless, but more large and
genial than his own.

Note 21, page 62.

Jacques Lefebvre of Etaples, in the diocese of
Amiens, was born about the middle of the fifteenth
century. He studied at Paris, and afterwards
travelled over a great part of Europe, and even
penetrated, according to some authorities, into
Asia and Africa. On his return to Paris, he was
appointed professor in the College of Cardinal
Lemoine, where he remained until 1507, when he
was introduced at court. In 1518, he was made
Bishop of Meaux. He was familiar with the
languages of classical antiquity, and had a fine and
critical taste in literature. For the old scholastic
system he had but little respect. He roused the
indignation of the Sorbonne by the publication of
a version of the New Testament with a comment-
ary. They were especially enraged at the horta-
tory discourse, in which he recommends the reading
of the Scriptures in the vulgar tongue to all the
faithful. The favour of Francis I. for a time protected him against the malice of his enemies ; but
he was at last obliged to take refuge in Strasburg.
On his return from his captivity in Madrid, Francis
appointed Lefebvre preceptor to his third son,

Charles ; and in this capacity he acquitted himself so well, that the king would have advanced him to the highest dignities in the church, had not his modesty led him to decline them. He spent his latter years with the Queen of Navarre at Nerac, and died in 1536. His life was exemplary, and his character frank and amiable.

Note 22, page 62.

Guillaume Cop was born at Basle, and prosecuted the study of medicine, first in his native town, and afterwards in Paris. He was principal physician to Louis XII. and Francis I. He was an accomplished scholar, and translated several of the writings of Hippocrates and Galen from the Greek. He died in 1532. His son *Nicolas* was professor in the College of Sainte-Barbe, and in 1533 was elected rector of the University of Paris. He was afterwards obliged to fly from Paris and take refuge in Basle, on account of a sermon which he preached, in order to refute the attacks directed by the Sorbonne against Marguerite of Navarre, who favoured and protected the doctrines and professors of Protestantism. This sermon is said to have been suggested, if not composed, by Calvin. *Rueil* was a learned physician of Soissons, born in 1497, died 1539. He wrote a treatise, ' *De Natura Stirpium.* '

Note 23, page 63.

Count Herman von Nuenar belonged to an ancient and noble German family, and was early imbued with a taste for literature by his relative Count Maurice von Spiegelberg, one of the illustrious band of scholars who went forth from the conventual seminary of St Agnes, near Zwoll in Westphalia, to restore and remodel the learning and education of Germany. Count Nuenar was provost of the archiepiscopal cathedral at Cologne, the headquarters of the enemies of Reuchlin. Yet he was a steady and warm friend to that great man. Like Erasmus, he attempted to steer a middle course between the Roman Catholic and Protestant parties.

Note 24, page 66.

This is but one instance out of many, of what was the peculiar and distinguishing characteristic of the genius of Ulrich von Hutten—a fearless, uncompromising love of truth and freedom, and an intense hatred of falsehood and tyranny.

Note 25, page 68.

On earth, that time never arrived for Hutten. His whole life was a struggle against religious and political abuses, against persecution, desertion, and disease; and to none of the great men of that

momentous sixteenth century would the motto—
afterwards assumed by Marnix de Sainte Alde-
gonde, the friend of the famous William the Silent
—'Repos ailleurs,' have better applied. But the
world owes most of the onward impulses which
have purified and improved it to men ill at ease.
The happy and the prosperous are too apt to confine themselves within the ancient limits.

Note 26, page 73.

Eoban Hess was born in 1488, in the village of
Bockendorff in Hesse, of poor parents. He early
manifested a decided talent for poetry, which was
assiduously cultivated ; and at Erfurth, where he
studied, he made the acquaintance, and acquired
the friendship, of Ulrich von Hutten. This friendship grew with their years, and continued till the
close of Hutten's short and brilliant career. They
laboured together to improve themselves, and to
enlighten their countrymen. Like Hutten, Hess
was intended for the law; but for that study he
showed a decided aversion, and devoted himself to
philology and poetry. In 1514 he married, and
soon afterwards was made rector of Erfurth. He
was a member of the deputation that welcomed
Luther on his journey to Worms. Pecuniary difficulties ultimately compelled him to leave Erfurth,
and he became teacher of the Gymnasium in

Nuremberg. He afterwards laboured in Marburgh, as professor for the diffusion of evangelical doctrine, and died in 1540. A life of him was published by Vossius, at Gotha, in 1797.

Note 27, page 73.

Sebastian von Rotenhan, a Franconian knight, was born in 1478. He was a man of considerable learning, and, like his brother knight, Eitelwolf von Stein, already mentioned, was fond of the study of history and antiquities. During the peasants' war, the Bishop of Halbertstadt entrusted him with the command of a castle, in which position he so distinguished himself, that a monument was erected, and a medal struck, in his honour. He travelled through many countries in Europe, visited Jerusalem, and was created a knight of the Holy Sepulchre. He was at various times entrusted with diplomatic negotiations, was a member of the Imperial Chamber at Costnitz, councillor to Albert, Archbishop of Mayence, and privy councillor to the Emperor Charles V. He died in 1542, at his castle of Rotweinsdorf.

Note 28, page 74.

The translation of the *Trias Romana*, here given by M. Chauffour-Kestner, is a mere summary of that searching and powerful satire. The original occupies seventy-three closely printed octavo pages of Münch's edition of the works of Hutten, printed at Berlin, in five volumes, 1821–5.

Note 29, page 89.

George of Freundsberg was one of the most celebrated of the German military adventurers of his time. He was exceedingly popular among the German mercenaries, and played an important part in the Italian wars, in which Bourbon and Pescara led the armies of Charles V. He commanded the German mercenaries at the battle of Pavia; and, in the motley army which Bourbon conducted to the sack of Rome in 1527, twelve thousand lanzknechts followed the banners of this daring partisan. Freundsberg was an ardent supporter of the Reformed doctrines, and a bitter enemy to the Church of Rome. He is said to have carried a silken cord in his pocket, for the purpose of strangling the Pope, if ever an opportunity presented itself, in a manner consistent with the pontifical dignity.

Note 30, page 93.

It seems probable that so accomplished a classical scholar as Hutten, while penning this indignant remonstrance against the tyranny of the Pope, must have had in view the famous burst of eloquence in which Cicero denounced the cruelties and tyranny

M

of Verres :—' *Facinus est vincire civem Romanum ;
scelus verberare ; prope parricidium necare : quid dicam
in crucem tollere ?*' To bind a Roman citizen, is a
crime ; to scourge him, an infamy ; to kill him, almost
a parricide ; but to crucify him, what shall I call it ?

Note 31, page 110.

Jerome Aleander was born in 1480, and was descended from a noble family in Istria. He possessed
great talents and learning ; but his passions were
violent, and his morality was of the laxest description. His acquaintance with the Hebrew language
was so accurate and extensive, that it gave colour
to Luther's allegation, that he was a Jew. He was,
besides, an accomplished classical scholar, and
master of several modern languages. In 1508,
Louis XII. appointed him professor of Philosophy
in the University of Paris ; and his success in that
capacity attracted the notice of the papal court,
ever anxious to appropriate the services of able,
adroit, and unscrupulous men. In 1519, Pope Leo
X. conferred upon Aleander the appointment of
librarian to the Vatican, and in 1520 sent him to
Germany to encounter, and, if possible, to dissipate
or avert, the storm which threatened the existence
of the Papacy. At the Diet of Worms, he under-
took the accusation of Luther, and made an elabo-
rate speech against him.

Note 32, page 112.

'In the matter of the Inquisition,' says Ranke, ' the Pope agreed to make the most important concessions. On the 21st October 1520, he declared to the Grand Inquisitor of Spain, that he would give no further encouragement to the demands of the Cortes of Arragon, that he would not confirm the briefs he had issued, and that he would introduce no innovation in the affairs of the Inquisition without the approbation of the Emperor. Even this did not satisfy Charles ; he demanded the entire revocation of the briefs. On the 12th of December, the Pope offered to declare all steps that had been taken against the Inquisition null and void. On the 16th January 1521, he at length actually permitted the Emperor to suppress the briefs, and expressed a wish to have them sent back to Rome, that he might annul them. . . . . How grievously were the hopes which such men as Hutten and Sickingen had placed on the young Emperor disappointed ! The papal Bull was executed without hesitation in the Low German hereditary dominions, where the higher clergy and confessors seemed to engross all the consideration of the court. In January 1521, there was a general belief that the Emperor wished to destroy Luther, and, if possible, to exterminate his followers.'

Note 33, page 126.

The *Fuggers* were the greatest bankers and
merchants in Germany, and were, in many respects,
to Augsburg what the Medici were to Florence,
though they never attained to the same height of
political power as their Italian contemporaries.
Both families sprung from a humble origin: the
Medici from an apothecary, the Fuggers from a
weaver.   John, who was the founder of the Fuggers,
lived in the early part of the fourteenth century.
But the Fuggers alluded to in the text, must have
been his descendants, Jacques, and his nephews
Raymond and Anthony.   Jacques for many years
directed the mercantile transactions of the house at
Venice and Augsburg.   At that period, in addition
to their other business, the Fuggers farmed the
gold mines in the valley of the Inn, and the silver
mines of Falkenstein and Schwartz.   In a single
year—1506—they made a profit of 175,000 ducats
from the sale of the merchandise imported by their
ships from the east.   Jacques built the magnificent
castle of Fuggerau; and, at the period of his death,
was knight of the Golden Spur, Count Palatine,
and Imperial Councillor.   His nephew Raymond
bought the county of Kirchberg from the Emperor,
for 525,000 florins.   He encouraged science and
literature, and formed a valuable library.   Both he

and his brother, however, seem to have been somewhat unscrupulous in their business transactions,
as we find that they were compelled to pay 60,000
ducats to the Queen of Hungary, in compensation
for the bad quality of the money which they had
coined, and with which they had inundated
Hungary. There appears, therefore, to have been
some foundation for the accusations brought against
them in the ' *Brigands.*' Raymond and Anthony
Fugger were often very useful to the Emperor
Charles V., when he was pressed for money. It is
related of them, that when that monarch lodged in
their palace, in passing through Augsburg, they
lighted the fire in his apartment with an acknow-
ledgment for 800,000 florins, with the imperial
signature attached. In return for the munificence
of the Fuggers, Charles rewarded them with
many valuable monopolies and privileges, such as
those of coining money in their towns and lordships,
and of being exempt from all judicial control, except that of the Emperor himself. Erasmus has
bestowed the highest praise on the character of
Anthony Fugger, with whom he was on terms of
intimate friendship. He appears to have been a
liberal patron of learning and the fine arts. He
paid Titian 3000 crowns for works executed at
Augsburg; collected the finest library that had
ever been formed in Germany; and founded and

endowed many charitable institutions, such as the Hospital of Waltenhausen. Yet, at his death, he left the enormous fortune of six millions of golden crowns, besides plate and jewels, large possessions in foreign countries, and factories at Antwerp and Venice. This explains the saying of Charles V., who exclaimed, on seeing the royal treasures at Paris, 'I have a single weaver in Augsburg, who could buy all this and pay for it with his own money.'

Note 34, page 130.

Rabulists—from the Latin *rabula*, a pettifogger, a noisy, wrangling advocate—is a term of reproach applied to those advocates who took advantage of their position for their own profit, instead of looking to the benefit of their clients, and who tried to deafen the judge, or overwhelm their opponents, by unnecessary clamour and violence.

Note 35, page 138.

John Ziska von Trocznow had lost an eye in childhood, whence he was surnamed Ziska, or the one-eyed. His sister, who was a nun, had been seduced by a priest; and this circumstance inspired him with the utmost hatred of the whole body of the priesthood. The doctrines of Huss, in spite of the murder of that Reformer in 1415, had spread rapidly throughout Bohemia; and Ziska put himself at the head of the movement, and gained repeated victories over the Imperialists and the Emperor Sigismund, who endeavoured to suppress it by force of arms. He lost his remaining eye at the siege of the castle of Raby; but still continued to lead his troops, and gain victories as before, in spite of his blindness. He died in October 1424, while advancing to invade Moravia. In person, Ziska was short and broad-shouldered, with a large, round, bald head. His forehead was deeply furrowed, and he wore long, fiery-red moustaches. After the loss of his eyes, he always rode in a carriage close to the great standard of the Hussite army. Knox probably borrowed his famous saying, ' That the best way to keep the rooks from returning, was to pull down their nests,' from that attributed in the text to the great general of the Hussites.

Note 36, page 139.

The following is the picture drawn by Menzel, in his History of Germany, of the state of the country at the close of the Thirty Years' War, which was terminated in 1648 by the Peace of Westphalia. ' Germany is reckoned by some to have lost one-half, by others two-thirds, of her entire population during the Thirty Years' War. In Saxony, 900,000 men had fallen within two years; in Bohemia, the number of inhabitants, at the demise of Ferdinand

II., before the last deplorable inroads made by
Banner and Tortenson, had sunk to one-fourth.
Augsburg, instead of eighty, had eighteen thousand
inhabitants. Every province, every town throughout the Empire, had suffered at an equal ratio, with
the exception of the Tyrol, which had repulsed the
enemy from her frontiers, and had enjoyed the
deepest peace during this period of horror. The
country was completely impoverished. The working class had almost totally disappeared. The
manufactories had been destroyed by fire, industry
and commerce had passed into other hands. The
products of Upper Germany were far inferior to
those of Italy and Switzerland, those of Lower
Germany to those of Holland and England. Immense provinces, once flourishing and populous, lay
entirely waste and uninhabited, and were only by
slow degrees repeopled by foreign emigrants, or
by soldiery. The original character and language
of the inhabitants were, by this means, completely
altered. In Franconia, which, owing to her central
position, had been traversed by every party during
the war, the misery and depopulation had risen to
such a pitch, that the Franconian Estates, with the
assent of the ecclesiastical princes, abolished (A.D.
1650) the celibacy of the Catholic clergy, and permitted each man to marry two wives, on account of
the numerical superiority of the women over the

men. The last remains of political liberty had, during the war, also been snatched from the people; each of the Estates had been deprived of the whole of its material power. The nobility were compelled by necessity to enter the service of the princes, the citizens were impoverished and powerless, the peasantry had been utterly demoralized by military rule and reduced to servitude. The provincial Estates, weakly guarded by the Crown against the encroachments of the petty princes, were completely at the mercy of the more powerful of the petty sovereigns of Germany, and had universally sunk in importance. Science and art had fled from Germany, and pedantic ignorance had replaced the deep learning of her universities. The mother tongue had become adulterated by an incredible variety of Spanish, Italian, and French words, and the use of foreign words with German terminations was considered the highest work of elegance. Various foreign modes of dress were also as generally adopted. Germany had lost all, save her hopes for the future.'

Note 37, page 141.

Well might the peasantry of that time regard with suspicion and detestation, anything that was likely to perpetuate and strengthen the crushing yoke of their feudal superiors, which is thus graphically described by M. Audin in his *Histoire de*

Luther. ' It was indeed a heavy oppression. At the death of the master of the family, the lord inherited his best pair of oxen; on that of the mistress, her best suit of clothes. This was the right of *Todfall.* Every peasant who changed masters, was obliged to pay a fine to the one he was leaving, the *Lehnschelling.* The finest bundle of wheat, the finest bunch of grapes, the finest fruits of his garden, the finest honey from his bees, all belonged to the lord. On Shrove Tuesday, he was bound to present him with a pig; on St Martin's day, with a couple of geese; at Michaelmas, with a couple of fowls. The temporal or spiritual lord treated his peasants like veritable slaves; body and mind, they were wholly subject to him; if he changed his religion, the vassal was compelled to go over with him to the new faith. With these were coupled the exactions of the priesthood, often as cruel and oppressive as those of the temporal lord.'

Note 38, page 147.

Dr Strauss places the date of Hutten's death a year earlier. According to him, he died towards the end of August or the beginning of September 1523, at the age of 35 years and 4 months.

INDEX.

MURRAY AND GIBB, PRINTERS, EDINBURGH.